C.J. SCOTT

SHEERAH

Female Builder of Towns in the Bronze Age

Acknowledgements

I GRATEFULLY THANK my family, Kingdom Writers Association, and especially the members of my critique group for their unflagging support and love. Thanks also to Brae and Jill Wyckoff.

Thank You Father, Son, and Holy Spirit!

DEDICATION

To my beloved granddaughter, Sophia,
with the sure knowledge that she can fulfill her destiny.

In the middle to late Bronze Age (fifteenth century B.C.), *"Ephraim's daughter was Sheerah, who built Upper Beth Horon, Lower Beth Horon, and Uzzam-Sheerah."* (Recorded in I Chronicles 7:24.)

CONTENTS

CHAPTER ONE

"**S**HEERAH!"

"YES, ABBA!" called the three-and-a-half-year-old. Her shiny black curls, wild as ever, bounced with the pat-pat-pat of her tiny bare feet as she came running to Ephraim's special room. On this occasion, her tiny hands, feet, and tunic were covered with black soot. He lifted her off her feet, holding her away from his robes.

"Where have you been? What have you been doing?" Ephraim asked with a chuckle.

"I building, Abba."

"Building with what?" he asked, amused.

"Rocks by fire. Eema cooks."

"Near the fire pit?" Ephraim wondered aloud. "Why not use the stones outside your play tent?"

"They falling."

"Where is your maid?"

At just that moment, Naamah, nursemaid to Sheerah, ran in, sliding into a curtsy before Ephraim. Out of breath, Naamah said, "I am sorry, my master," without delay.

"Here." Ephraim held the squirmy little girl out to her maid, trying to avoid getting soot on his robes.

Naamah smiled as she left with Sheerah. "You and your buildings," Naamah said as she shook her head.

Sheerah wiggled away, saying, "I build a town. I show you." Her deep brown eyes, fringed with black lashes, glittered with enthusiasm.

"First, we need to get you cleaned up."

Naamah took her unwilling charge, wiggling all the way, to the back of the house on the second floor. She located the jar with the dregs of the last olive oil pressing. It was not edible, but it was still too valuable to discard. A second jar revealed sand, pounded almost to a powder. Naamah removed Sheerah's tunic, shaking her head again. The little girl's skin would get clean, but the tunic would need to be washed in the river. Naamah was not sure she could get the soot out, even after much beating on the rocks. Luckily, Sheerah had other tunics. Still, Naamah knew she would need to make Sheerah a new one soon, *slightly larger size*, she noted with satisfaction.

Sheerah continued running all over the upper-level tile floor, leaving sooty footprints everywhere she stepped. With a planned move, Naamah grabbed Sheerah as she ran by, causing the little one to squeal. And then the cleaning began.

Dipping her fingers in the oil, Naamah rubbed it on Sheerah's skin; then she poured the fine sand into her hand and rubbed it over the oil. The soot came off almost like magic. As the sand released, the soot went with it, leaving Sheerah's skin looking like burnished bronze. A clean tunic finished the process.

"C'mon," Sheerah insisted, "let's go see!" She wiggled herself free, grabbing Naamah's hand and dragging her toward the cooking fire area. Off to one side, little piles of square coals were lined up along a "road" made of a scratch in the dirt. With a slight bow, Naamah said to Shuai, Sheerah's mother, "Have you seen this?" She pointed to Sheerah's "town" with a smile. Shuai smiled and nodded.

CHAPTER TWO

THE MIDDAY HEAT was oppressive as Naamah ground the grain for the family. She felt sleepy, but not for long. Piercing screams rent the noonday air. *Where was Sheerah?* she thought. *She had been here a minute ago.* Naamah ran in the direction of the screams, panicked. Rounding a large outcropping of rocks, she was horrified to see Sheerah in a heap on the sand.

Naamah cried out and ran to the little girl, just as the malicious, triangular head of an adder slithered away. Its bronze and gold spotted body moved toward the rocks. Sheerah was still breathing, but in very shallow little puffs, while her leg had become grotesquely swollen near the hideous snake bite. Heart in her mouth with icy fear, Naamah picked up the little girl and began running back to the house. About halfway back, she was met by Aaron and another male servant who heard the screams and came running. Aaron took Sheerah from Naamah, and seeing her condition, shook his head with sadness.

Adder bites were invariably fatal.

They put Sheerah in her bed, and Naamah tied a rag very tightly around her leg above the bite wound. She was already a little feverish. Sheerah's parents were not returning until the

3

following morning—*oo late*, Naamah thought. *She would be dead by then.*

Naamah sobbed over the little girl, devastated. Her hands shook as she tried to think of something to do for her master's child, a child she loved as her very own.

"Pray," said a still, small voice.

What? Naamah thought. She looked around. *Who is speaking to me?? Oh, what good would that do anyway?* The house servants had already called on their various gods for help, with no response.

"Pray to the God of the child's father," the voice came again.

The invisible One – what could He do? Could He really help the little girl in this dire situation? Why would He help them? Just then, Sheerah cried out in pain. She was awake now, but the mottled area around the snake bite wound was starting to turn black and smell foul. She moaned and rolled from side to side in pain. Naamah wished there was something she could do to ease her suffering.

Naamah felt embarrassed but decided to answer the still, small voice anyway. *What to say? What name should she use? She understood the household gods liked hearing about themselves and how great they were.*

She decided to start with that. Sheerah was moaning more loudly and calling for her abba.

"God of my master, Ephraim, please hear me. You are great, and my master trusts you. Please help my little Sheerah. Take my life in her place. Don't let her die. Thank you for hearing my prayer."

She didn't know what else to say. She sobbed herself to sleep sitting on the floor next to Sheerah's bed.

CHAPTER THREE

T HE NEXT MORNING, as the warm sun filled the house with light, Naamah woke up expecting the worst. She looked over at Sheerah. She was no longer moaning and rolling side to side. Sheerah's sweaty hair was plastered to her face. When she saw her, Naamah's first thought was that Sheerah had died during the night. She leaned over the little girl, startled to see that the discolored, necrotic skin was gone. Sheerah's leg was still red, but her fever was gone. Naamah was overjoyed but mystified. She had never heard of a person surviving more than a day after an adder bite, and Sheerah was so small for the amount of venom the snake surely released into her body.

Was this Ephraim's God answering her prayer?

There was a commotion in the yard. Ephraim and Shuai had returned from their travels to inspect the herds and flocks. The household servants broke the devastating news to them about Sheerah. Shuai screamed and almost fainted. Ephraim caught her before she could fall. Sheerah's parents raced up the narrow stairway to the second level of the house. They first encountered Naamah, who sat by the bed, obviously nervous, but smiling broadly. They made their way over to Sheerah's bed. The little girl was not only alive, but she was also smiling at them. She was quite weak, but obviously getting better.

Ephraim looked at Naamah and said, "The servants said it was an adder bite. How then is she still alive? Are you sure it was an adder?"

"Yes, my master, I saw it clearly. I must speak to you and my mistress in private, so I can tell you what happened."

Ephraim asked all the servants to leave. Naamah was so excited she could hardly speak.

"I did all I could to make her comfortable and put a tight band around her leg above the bite wound, but she was getting worse and worse. The servants prayed, and the wise woman from the village came and prayed also. Nothing helped. I heard a soft voice telling me to pray to your God, master, so I did."

Ephraim looked shocked and afraid. Only the priests could pray to Almighty God, and then only on holy days. Would He really listen to a servant girl about his daughter and answer? How else to explain his daughter's recovery from certain death? Ephraim was very puzzled.

"I must speak with the priest as soon as possible," he said as he turned and headed toward the temple to offer sacrifices.

When Ephraim explained the events of the previous day to the priest, he was as mystified as Ephraim. He told Ephraim that he would study with the elders, who knew the oral traditions of their people intimately. Not one of them had any recollection of a similar healing in the past. The priest decided to thank and praise God anyway.

CHAPTER FOUR

S HEERAH'S BIRTHDAY—SUCH EXCITEMENT! When a child survived to age six, it was considered a cause for much celebration. Many children did not survive past their fifth year. Accidents and childhood diseases claimed many as they grew up. Sheerah's upcoming birthday celebration was especially poignant after the snake bite incident.

Sheerah was turning six.

She was very excited. There will be lots of gifts, good food, her cousins coming by, and her first camel ride. She could hardly stand still, hopping from one foot to the other.

It did not seem possible, but the level of joy was increased by news brought by the men who guarded the perimeter of Ephraim's vast lands. They were laughing as they told of a caravan headed in the direction of Ephraim's small collection of family homes. This did not happen often, but the stories told by members of the tribe around the campfires at night were fascinating to Sheerah.

The oral history of her people.

They told of traders carrying spices, silks, and other valuable fabrics, jewels, perfumes, utensils, and tools for the home; they also brought delicious food. Many things Sheerah had never even dreamed about made her squeal with excitement.

"I can't wait! I've heard so many stories!" Sheerah almost shouted. Tasty things Sheerah had never even dreamed about were about to flood her home. She especially wanted to taste the honeyed dates that her older cousins were talking about.

Sheerah heard and then smelled the caravan as it arrived. Exotic smells and colorfully decorated camels covered with bells. A few decorated carts came over the hill with the camels. They were covered with tiny bells and shiny pieces of metal. Sheerah was so excited, she could hardly breathe. She wanted to run everywhere and see everything. Naamah kept holding her back, and Sheerah was getting very frustrated. Naamah had explained to her several times that the merchants and their musical and beautiful camels sometimes took children to be sold as slaves. Naamah would stay very close.

Eventually, the bedlam subsided as the traders settled their camels for the night. They camped on Ephraim's land and were shown where to get water for themselves and their animals.

The pinks, purples, and blues of dawn were still decorating the horizon when Sheerah began pestering Naamah to go to see the caravan.

"Naamah, wake up!" Sheerah implored. Naamah, still sleepy, rolled over and feigned sleep. When that did not work, she groaned. Sheerah promptly jumped up on her bed and grabbed her tired nursemaid, but Naamah knew that once Sheerah was awake, there was no chance of going back to sleep.

"Sheerah, stop jumping on me!" she grumbled.

"So, you *are* awake!" Sheerah said with an accusing tone. "I want to see the caravan! Hurry up!"

"Believe me," Naamah said, yawning, "no one in the caravan is awake yet." "You need your morning meal first anyway."

"Okay," Sheerah pouted. Before Naamah could stop her, Sheerah ran to her mother's room. Shuai was still asleep, and Sheerah was surprised to see Ephraim asleep beside her. He usually slept in his own house. Seeing him there, Sheerah backed out of the room.

Pat, pat, pat went her small feet on the cool tile as she hurried back to her own room.

Naamah soon arrived with a steaming bowl of barley porridge, one of Sheerah's favorites. She hoped to distract the little girl from her desired objective—seeing the caravan. It didn't work. Naamah knew there would not be much activity until the cool of the evening, but she also knew Sheerah would not be dissuaded.

Such a tenacious child, Naamah thought, smiling. She stalled for time, getting herself and Sheerah dressed.

"C'mon,". Sheerah pleaded. Hurry up!"

"Okay, okay, I'm coming."

One of the male household servants would accompany them. He would be with them to protect them from any trouble and to carry Sheerah when she got tired. At six years old, she was still too heavy for Naamah to carry very far, regardless of her slight frame.

They walked and walked.

And walked.

Sheerah began to wonder if she had imagined the sights, sounds, and smells of the previous evening. It was less than a mile, but a long way for an excited six-year-old. As they rounded an outcropping of rock, they were assaulted by wonderful fragrances.

"See, I told you it wasn't too early," Sheerah said in a petulant tone. Naamah just smiled. Sheerah stopped in her tracks, almost tripping Naamah. "What are those?" Sheerah said with fear and a little incredulity in her voice.

Naamah looked up to see some large creatures being led by a boy about Sheerah's age. They weren't as big as the camels but still impressive in size. Naamah had only seen them once before and was having trouble remembering what they were called.

Suddenly, she remembered. "Horses," she told Sheerah. "That's what they are called." *Somebody very wealthy was traveling with this caravan,* she mused.

The boy leading the horses stopped suddenly, staring at Sheerah. When their eyes met, she smiled and then fingered her necklace and touched the frontlet ornament on her forehead. Naamah insisted that she wear the jewelry today, and she was glad because she felt shy. After a moment, Sheerah looked at the ground.

There was a shout from the caravan's living area, and the boy went on his way, leading the horses to the watering trough. Sheerah was fascinated with the horses and pestered Naamah for more information about them.

"They seem gentle, following that boy like that," Sheerah decided. "I'd like to ask that boy some questions."

"No, you cannot go over there; it's dangerous," Naamah said with a seldom-heard sternness in her voice. "We can come back later this evening when more people will be about. I know your eema wants some new, pretty fabric. Perhaps she will make you a new tunic or something. It is also time to gather cloth for your bride's clothing." A bride's adornment took years to complete. Multi-colored embroidery, small bells, and jewels would be attached as part of her dowry.

"Well, I want some honeyed figs," Sheerah said with enthusiasm.

"All right."

They returned to the house and rested during the intense heat of the day. But Ephraim's household was abuzz with excitement for the coming evening when they would visit the caravan.

CHAPTER FIVE

E VERYONE, INCLUDING EPHRAIM, was in a jovial mood. Sheerah saw him give a small coin to each of his most trusted servants so they could celebrate at the caravan too. *The evening meal was light but took forever,* Sheerah thought.

Finally, the procession to the caravan area began. Ephraim and Shuai led the way, followed by Ephraim's other wives, then the trusted servants, including Naamah with Sheerah in tow. Sheerah hopped from one foot to the other, running little circles around Naamah, even jumping up and down. She could scarcely contain her excitement. A sharp word from Shuai and a look from Ephraim settled her a bit. Naamah explained," You are Ephraim's daughter, and you need to act like it."

"But why is he so slow?" Sheerah whined.

"He is an important person, so he walks slowly, very dignified. The traders who travel with the caravan must be aware that they need to respect his leadership.

Up ahead, the area where the caravan had settled was ablaze with light. Family groups gathered around large cooking fires. There were burning lamps suspended from the tent poles, making everything seem to sparkle. They finally arrived at the entrance to the caravan's temporary settlement. Sheerah was so excited, she started jumping again. Uh-oh! More waiting!

Ephraim and Shuai greeted the leaders of the caravan tribe. This was taking so long! Sheerah could hardly keep her feet still, but did her best to stand quietly next to Naamah.

Someone is watching me, Sheerah thought. She looked around just in time to see the boy who had the horses jump behind a tent. *Why does he keep looking at me?* she wondered. Tugging on her nurse, she asked, "Naamah, where are the horses?"

"Ah, what did you ask me, Sheerah?"

Naamah was also having trouble concentrating. The intoxicating aromas, sparkling gems, tin, and copper for making bronze, were quite overwhelming. She stared at the women dressed in their finest embroidered clothing, the bolts of silk, and other fabrics with their multiple colors and textures.

"I want to see the horses, where are they?" Sheerah asked with a note of petulance in her tone.

Naamah knew she should correct her, but she felt like a child herself. "Let's go look for them, but you must stay with me," she cautioned Sheerah. Let's start over this way with those carts.

The traders displayed their wares with care. Naamah was interested in looking at everything, but Sheerah pulled on her hand every time she paused. Naamah knew that nothing else would satisfy Sheerah until they found the horses. *And the boy who was leading them,* she thought with a smile.

Naamah caught a whiff of camel dung. It would make sense to keep the animals all in the same area. She headed toward the camel smell. As she did, she found a second camp coming into view. Spacious tents sprawled with incredible, beautifully decorated rugs spilling out of the entrances. Painted lamps lit the area, and Naamah was certain that this was the wealthy family she had imagined before. They must be traveling with the caravan for safety. The horses should be around here somewhere.

And, of course, Sheerah had found them.

She was no longer dancing around impatiently. Instead, she was staring at the boy she had seen earlier. Sheerah wanted to ask him about the horses, but felt suddenly shy.

Sheerah and Naamah were approached by a lovely lady dressed in embroidered silk clothing. Naamah bowed before this obviously wealthy and important person. She was glad to see that Sheerah imitated her and bowed. The lady smiled her approval.

"I am Abigail," she said. "Welcome to my home."

"This is Sheerah, daughter of Ephraim," Naamah responded, "I am her servant and yours."

"Please come in and join me for some tea," Abigail suggested, looking at Sheerah and smiling.

"Thank you," Sheerah replied politely.

Naamah nodded, and they followed Abigail into the largest of the tents. The rugs were the softest thing Sheerah had ever walked on. She was uncharacteristically speechless at the beauty around them. There were pillows everywhere, and they looked like they were made of silk.

Pillows of silk, Sheerah wondered. *Was that possible?*

Abigail sat gracefully on a giant, striped pillow. She indicated that Sheerah and Naamah should also sit. There were no chairs, just pillows. When Sheerah sat on one of the pillows, she was amazed at the softness. Just then, a servant brought in tea on a bronze tray. It looked like the cups were made of bronze, too. The hot tea was incredibly good, and Sheerah was surprised that it was sweet and that the teacups, though bronze, did not burn her fingers. Sheerah thought, *I have never tasted anything so good.*

Abigail was kind and asked Sheerah some questions about her family. Naamah was immensely proud of the way Sheerah was handling this unexpected situation. Sheerah was calm, but

Naamah knew her charge was a ball of questions inside her good manners.

Unable to contain her curiosity, Sheerah asked, "Do you have horses?"

"Yes, we do. Are you the girl my son saw this morning?"

"He told you about that?" Sheerah inquired, feeling shy again.

"Yes, he did," Abigail said with a twinkle in her eye. "Would you like to meet him? He can show you the horses." She called out," Zeruiah, come in here, please." Almost as soon as she called out, a boy about Sheerah's age peeked in through the back of the tent. He was dressed in fine clothes. He looked so much different from the work clothes of earlier in the day. Zeruiah's tunic was a deep purple, belted with a bronze buckled belt. Sheerah didn't notice anything except his dark curly hair. "Zeruiah, this is Sheerah."

"Hello, Sheerah," he said, bowing.

Sheerah thought she should bow, but she was already seated on a pillow. So she scrambled to her feet.

Abigail said, "Sheerah is extremely interested in the horses. Would you please show them to her?"

They walked in silence across the camp, followed by a servant and Naamah, to an undecorated tent. *Do the horses have their own tent?* Sheerah thought. *Amazing!* As they entered the tent, she heard Zeruiah speak softly to the horses. There were four of them. Three of them were various colors of brown, and one was a light tan or gold. They smelled of grass and sunshine. There were flies around, but Sheerah scarcely noticed. The nearest horse turned to face him, and Zeruiah petted its nose. The horse did not try to bite or spit like the camels she had seen.

"May I pet him like you did?" Sheerah requested.

"Sure," Zeruiah said. "But you mustn't be afraid. They can sense fear and may try to bite or push you."

Sheerah worked up her courage and walked right up to the brown horse. The horse lowered his large head, and she petted him on the nose. His nose was incredibly soft and smooth. Sheerah was entranced but also sad because she knew she would probably never see or pet him again.

"Sheerah!" came Naamah's worried call from just inside the tent flap. The male servant had been close the entire time, but Naamah was afraid of the horses.

Sheerah said, "I guess I must go. Thank you for showing me the horses. I will never forget this night."

Naamah and Sheerah hurried back to the main camp. Naamah was carrying a message for Ephraim.

CHAPTER SIX

THOUGH NAAMAH CONSIDERED her message for Ephraim especially important, it would need to be communicated after Sheerah went to sleep. She was clearly still excited by the caravan, and especially Zeruiah and the horses. When the little girl finally fell asleep, Naamah went to Ephraim's house to give him Abigail's message.

"Ephraim, I have a message from Abigail for you," Naamah began as she curtsied, seeking entrance to Ephraim's chamber.

Shuai was sitting quietly in the corner.

"Who is Abigail?" Ephraim interrupted.

Naamah replied, "The widow of a very wealthy man who had no brothers. Her servants told me the story. She was married young to a wealthy, older man. Against all odds, it was a love match. She struggled with apparent infertility until God blessed them with one son, Zeruiah. Mattias shared all kinds of knowledge with Abigail, including the management and increase of their wealth, until he became sick and died. Abigail was devastated. She remained unmarried to manage her husband's vast holdings and finances until Zeruiah was of age. Her family is traveling with the caravan for safety."

"The people with horses, right?" he replied. "Now what could this message be? " looking at Naamah.

"She was very impressed with Sheerah when we had tea with her. She wants to meet with you two to discuss a possible joining of the two families with a wedding between Sheerah and her son, Zeruiah," Naamah confided.

Shuai started to object, "She's only six!"

"It will soon be time to find her a husband. We will talk to Abigail," Ephraim said firmly.

Ephraim told Naamah," Make arrangements to join Abigail in her tents for dinner.

"Yes, my master," Naamah said humbly.

That day, Shuai was extremely excited and spent the afternoon trying to decide what to wear. She finally decided on a royal blue fitted tunic, covered by a shawl of greens, purples, and blues. It was important to her that Abigail understand that Ephraim was a great leader among the tribes of what would become Israel. These colored robes held great significance for that fact to be known. Having his daughter in her family would be an incredibly special privilege for Abigail and the tribe to which she belonged.

Ephraim looked regal in his finest tunic with several layers of robes. He and Shuai arrived just about sunset, in sedan chairs at Abigail's encampment, with several servants in their entourage. They were greeted by Abigail's personal servant dressed in fine clothes.

"My mistress is honored by your visit. Please come in," said the servant with a bow. Shuai was stunned by the opulence of the drapes, furnishings, and multicolored pillows, large and small.

Before Shuai could comment on the beauty, Abigail appeared at the other side of the spacious tent. She was dressed in a beautiful silk tunic with embroidery and jewels all over it.

As darkness fell, there were many lamps lit within the tent. Some had a crystal in front of them that made the light sparkle. The scent of a lovely incense filled the large room.

Abigail bowed to Ephraim and then greeted Shuai warmly by grasping her hand with both of Abigail's. Shuai took a quick glance at Ephraim and was pleased to see that he, too, was impressed. They felt hopeful. She had to smile as she realized that no outsider would ever know how he was affected. But as his number one and favorite wife, she had known him for an exceptionally long time.

"Thank you for coming to my home," Abigail spoke for the first time. "You look lovely, Shuai."

"We are honored to be your guests," Ephraim said with appropriate solemnity.

Abigail sank gracefully into a group of silk and satin pillows. She indicated, with an inviting wave of her arm, that Shuai and Ephraim should sit in the group of pillows near her.

Immediately, a servant brought in tea and sweets on a bronze tray.

"Dinner will be served shortly," Abigail said.

"I am sure it will be delicious," Ephraim remarked.

As they had traveled to Abigail's encampment, he and Shuai had been discussing what might be served. Ephraim expected salted fish, and Shuai was hoping for some new kinds of bread.

With a clap of Abigail's hands, a small parade of servants came in carrying trays of all kinds of food. The first servant had small bronze trays for each diner. Some servants carried fancy skins of wine. Shuai noted with approval that a few of the smaller serving pieces were made of bronze. This was another testimony to Abigail's wealth. A servant came behind the diners and placed a cloth on the lap of each one. Each servant in turn came closer to Ephraim, Shuai, and Abigail, serving them something from the tray he or she carried.

There was a plethora of types of food and sweets. Roasted meat of several varieties, exotic dried fruits, and several varieties of dates dripping with honey. Goat cheese graced several of the trays of dates. There was also salted fish, to Ephraim's delight, and some small, curled fish called shellfish. They had individual shells and little, tiny feet.

Fascinating, thought Shuai.

Noticing Shuai's interest, Abigail said, "The caravan has many opportunities to buy new things.

"These are delicious as is everything. What a lovely dinner!" said Shuai, full of pleasure at such a banquet.

The time for serious negotiating had come. Joining two large families and territories was no easy task.

"My daughter will bring an excellent dowry with her to her marriage.", Ephraim stated confidently.

"I think you will find our bride price satisfactory," Abigail stated with certainty.

"Sheerah will bring fine linens, five sets of clothing, her family jewels, two servants, and 200 heads of sheep."

"It is a kind offer," Abigail said shrewdly, "but we have no need for more sheep. Some of your goats with the soft coats would be appreciated. They are known throughout the region for their fine fiber, which can be spun into warm yarn."

"They are far more valuable than sheep for their milk in addition to the fiber. I would offer 50 goats as part of the dowry." Ephraim stated.

"The bride price will be four servants—well-trained, an excellent shepherd, one pound of jewels, two talents of gold, and one horse," Abigail finished with a flourish.

"While the horse is indeed interesting, I do not have any horses to breed with, and two camels would be much more useful to me," said Ephraim.

Shuai thought, *I hope Sheerah does not find out that Ephraim rejected the offer of a horse. Although, once she is married, she will have the opportunity to be around the* horses.

"Two camels it is. I am very anxious to join our two families."

As a wife, Shuai knew she was to be silent during these

negotiations, but could not hold her tongue any longer and said, "You do realize she is only six years old?"

Abigail smiled kindly and said, "Of course, I would expect that the wedding would not be for another seven or eight years. But, to seal our agreement, the bride price will be paid immediately."

"That will be satisfactory, and the dowry will come with Sheerah at the time of the wedding."

"You are a shrewd negotiator," Abigail said with a small smile. "I accept."

CHAPTER SEVEN

THE NIGHT WAS balmy and beautiful as Shuai and Ephraim made their way back to Shuai's home, as Ephraim had promised to stay the night. Ephraim was uncharacteristic in his generosity to his wives. Each wife had her own dwelling. In his quiet manner, Ephraim did not say much. But the small smile on his lips let Shuai know he was satisfied with this night's business.

It seems like a good match, thought Shuai. *Why is my heart so restless? Is it because Sheerah is so young, or is it that my little girl is growing up? What do we really know about Abigail? She is wealthy, no doubt, having hired a large caravan to travel with. Is her son kind?* She chided herself. *No point in dreaming of a happy, carefree life.* She turned over in bed again, careful not to wake Ephraim. Sleep was elusive for the remainder of the night. In the morning, Shuai would get out the bridal decorations and jewelry she had created for Sheerah. It was time to get busy.

Shuai and Ephraim agreed not to tell Sheerah right away. *She has a lot to learn about being a wife and running a household,* Shuai thought. She said aloud to Ephraim, "Today Naamah will teach Sheerah how we bake bread."

But Sheerah had no such grown-up thoughts. She wanted to go back to the caravan today.

"Naamah, I need to go back to the caravan today."

"What for?" came the short response.

"I want to buy a surprise for Eema."

"What are you going to use to buy that something?" Naamah asked with a smile.

"My abba gives me everything I need. I'll just ask him."

"It's dangerous," Naamah replied. "We can't go alone."

"Can we go with Aaron again?" Sheerah entreated.

"You stay here, I'll get permission from Ephraim and ask for the use of Aaron's assistance." (Aaron was one of Ephraim's most trusted slaves and often did family protection duty). "It shouldn't be a problem to have him as an escort today. Do not move, Sheerah. I'll be back very soon."

Sheerah sat on a chair, kicking her feet. Then she got up and went across the room to the other chair and sat. She began to squirm until she was backward in the chair. She turned back around. She got up and walked across the room, kicking her feet again. She looked out the door, and, still not seeing Naamah, sighed and went back to her original chair.

Naamah, for her part, was making her errand take as long as possible. She was afraid to go back to the caravan. Something she couldn't quite identify was bothering her. She arrived at Ephraim's room and curtsied in the doorway. He noticed her and motioned for her to come into the room. As she approached his big chair, she kept her eyes downcast.

"What has Sheerah done now?" he asked with an indulgent chuckle.

"Nothing, my master," she said tentatively. "It's what she wants to do that I need to discuss with you."

"What is it?"

"She wants to go back to the caravan to purchase a surprise for her eema."

Ephraim laughed aloud. "And what is she planning to do her purchasing with?"

Naamah looked up and said, "She says her Abba always gives her what she needs and wants. Also, we need Aaron to go with us," she finished in a rush.

Ephraim agreed.

Naamah returned to Sheerah to give her the good news. Sheerah was very excited, but Naamah told her she must wait for the following day. Sheerah had a restless night, since she was so excited about her mission.

Early in the morning, Sheerah and Naamah joined Aaron at the front of Ephraim's house. Naamah couldn't shake the feeling of foreboding she had about their venture.

Sheerah, on the other hand, was in high spirits, talking nonstop. They walked along with Aaron in his proper position, two to three yards behind them. The skies had an ominous tone to them. Yellow and bronze colors seemed to mix with the blue. Naamah hurried them along, hoping to finish the errand and get back to their home before...

Before what, she asked herself.

They arrived at the entrance to the caravan's space, breathless from their pace. The wonderful aromas, beautiful sights, and sounds of the caravan's wares soon captured Naamah's attention,and she forgot about her misgivings. Sheerah seemed to know exactly what she was seeking, but finding it was another matter due to the number of carts and vendors. Naamah had asked her what she was looking for half a dozen times. Her only answer had been "blue."

Sheerah refused to be satisfied until she found exactly what she was looking for.

Cart to cart and vendor to vendor, Sheerah searched diligently. Since she was so young, many vendors ignored her until Naamah walked up. Finally, a squeal from Sheerah caught Naamah's attention. She had found what she had been seeking.

There, in the display, was a lovely piece of lapis lazuli. It was set in bronze, making a bold yet ethereal pendant. It was a beautiful present for Shuai from her daughter. *I hope I have enough money to pay for it,* Naamah thought.

And they almost didn't. She bargained with the vendor, finally resorting to an emotional plea that Sheerah was so young and wanted the pendant as a gift for her eema. The vendor gave in and let them purchase it for half price.

Looking up at the ominous sky, Naamah said, "We'd better get home in a hurry."

Sheerah had eyes for nothing except her prize.

Chapter Eight

THE WIND WAS picking up in intensity, and Naamah became truly concerned. The misgivings of earlier came back to haunt her. All of a sudden, she realized that Aaron was no longer with them. *Great, just great. Aaron, of all the household servants, is usually so conscientious when watching over Sheerah and me,* Naamah thought. *But he is nowhere to be seen.*

The wind was now picking up little swirls of sand around their feet and ankles.

"Hurry, little Sheerah, we need to run," Naamah said.

She was glad she had convinced Sheerah to put the treasure in her bag instead of carrying it herself. In a matter of moments, the wind had become so much stronger. Naamah began looking fruitlessly for a place to shelter them, but unfortunately, all she could see was sand and small rocks. The wind seemed to be howling, and they didn't know which way to go. Bits of sand stung their skin like a million tiny biting insects. Naamah could no longer fight the wind and hang onto Sheerah. Without Aaron and no shelter, the safest thing she could do was cover her charge. Naamah just sat down and pulled Sheerah into her lap, doing her best to cover them both with her shawls. Sheerah squirmed because the heat and blowing sand made it difficult to breathe. All around them was the red-yellow flying sand, but Naamah squeezed her as tight and close as possible for as long as possible. As the storm raged on, Naamah realized that she and her precious Sheerah could die in this sandstorm. They could be covered with sand, suffocate, and never be found.

"*Pray,*" said the small voice inside her.

She had not heard that gentle sound since the snakebite incident. *Do I dare ask again?* she thought. *I don't care what happens to me, but my heart breaks for this young girl with me. Should I pray in my mind? Nothing can be heard above this screaming wind, anyway.*

Naamah opted to pray without moving her mouth. *Lord God of my master Ephraim,* she implored, *please have pity on his daughter, as you did before. We need help! Please save us from this storm!* She prayed earnestly, but she was still full of fear. Ephraim himself had told her that only the priests may pray to Almighty God, and she didn't want to get into trouble. The wind seemed to grow even louder, as if answering her. *Please God, save Your daughter,* she prayed with her mind. *You can take my life in her place.*

"Oof!" Naamah said with a groan as something punched her in the back. She couldn't see anything, but in a moment, Aaron's face appeared above her, surrounded by the howling sand. He had literally tripped over them while searching for them in the storm, which was powerful, but less intense than a while ago. Naamah was so glad to see him, and he used the camel to shelter them from the remnants of the storm.

Soon, all became quiet as the wind died away as quickly as it had arisen. Sheerah jumped up, shook off as much sand as she could, and then looked around. The desert, as far as she could see, was completely flat except for the little mound she and Naamah had created with Aaron and the camel. Naamah smiled, once again curious about the blessing.

Was that You, God of my master? How else did Aaron remain

on his feet and stumble across us? From that moment. Naamah was convinced that Ephraim's God really did exist and, unbelievably, did answer prayers—even hers.

Aaron, Naamah, and Sheerah eventually arrived home, exhausted. Ephraim and Shuai were both relieved and overjoyed to see them. They could see the storm ravaging the marketplace and didn't know if Sheerah and Naamah were caught in it.

Unfazed by everyone's response to the storm, Sheerah walked up to her mom. She shyly gave Eema the jewel from the caravan.

"Is this what you went back to the caravan for?" Shuai looked from Sheerah to Naamah and back to Sheerah. When her daughter nodded, they both began to cry.

"You could have died when that storm came up. *You* are the best gift I could ever hope for." Shuai held up her gift. "But this," she said, "is lovely!"

"I wanted something special for you, and when I saw it at the caravan," Sheerah said, "I knew it was perfect. "

Shuai looked at Ephraim and then over to Naamah. This was an expensive piece, and Naamah needed to be reimbursed.

This would be beautiful for Sheerah's wedding, Shuai thought. *But there will be time enough for those preparations later.*

CHAPTER NINE

THE DAY FOLLOWING their harrowing experience in the sandstorm, Naamah and Sheerah set about making bread. Sheerah was, as usual, curious and questioned everything. So, Naamah decided to show her the steps to making bread from the very beginning.

"Sheerah," Naamah prompted, "let's go to the storage area upstairs and get the grain for the bread you will be making." It was a quick walk, and Naamah tried to show Sheerah how important it was to be focused by the way she gathered the grains. It almost worked.

"Naamah, why do we need grains from two different jars?" Sheerah asked, peering inside over the edge of the large storage jars.

"Using wheat and barley together makes the bread taste better. It's your Abba's favored choice. Besides, we may have some barley left over to make your favorite porridge." But Sheerah wasn't listening. Already, her eyes were on some new item.

"What is this?" Sheerah asked, holding out a clay bowl with perforations in it.

Naamah smiled and said, "That is for making your Abba's

favorite barley beer, which I will teach you another day. Put it back carefully, please."

"Yes, Naamah," Sheerah said as she turned to put the container back in its place.

They proceeded downstairs and out the back door. The little table and stool were ready for the process of grinding the grain.

"This is the quern," Naamah explained. "Sit down here on the stool."

"What's this?" Sheerah asked as she picked up the rock sitting on top. She was surprised by its lack of weight.

"That is called the maso. The stone attached to the table is the metate."

Sheerah tried saying the unusual names, as if to memorize them. "Why is the maso so bumpy? It is very rough."

"That's what helps us grind the grain."

"It's not very heavy for a rock this size."

Naamah said, "You will be glad of that by the time we get done." She rose. "Let's go light the fire in the oven, so it will be ready when we need it."

The squat, small, round oven was a short distance from the house. Sheerah helped Naamah load the dried manure into the depression below the oven. Naamah took a stick from the ever-present cooking fire to light it. The manure would burn down while they made the bread, and the oven would be at a moderate temperature by the time they put the bread in.

Naamah poured some of the grain from each jar onto the metate. She showed Sheerah the back-and-forth movement of the maso that ground the grain into coarse flour.

"Now you try, Sheerah," Naamah said, encouraging her.

As expected, Sheerah was clumsy at first, and the grain seemed to be winning.

"Argh!" Sheerah almost shouted in her frustration. "I can't do this!"

"Don't be so hard on yourself," Naamah said as she took the maso from Sheerah. By the look on her face, the maso was in danger of being thrown. "Let me show you again."

"I want to go *build* something," said Sheerah. "I know I can do that."

Naamah patiently demonstrated again. "I have an idea: put your hands on the maso, and I will put my hands on yours. That way, you can get a feel for it."

They worked for a bit, then Sheerah bent down and looked at their product. It was as fine as when Naamah did it herself. They took a small brush of camel hair and brushed the flour into a mixing tray. Then Sheerah stood up.

"Hey, where do you think you're going?" Naamah questioned.

"We made flour," Sheerah said with confidence. "I'm done and I'm going to build something."

"Not so fast, my girl!" Naamah replied. "No one is going to enjoy eating plain flour. We need to grind some more flour and then mix the bread." As she said this, she dumped more wheat and barley on the metate.

Sheerah groaned and picked up the maso. Her second solo attempt was more successful, but still a little grainy. *How does Naamah do this all the time?* Sheerah wondered to herself. *How does she grind the grain so finely?*

"Sheerah, please pay attention. We're ready for the next step."

What is she going to do with those roots? She contemplated. *Uh oh, she's carrying another rock—what now?*

"Put these in the mixing tray, Sheerah. Take this rock and smash them to get the liquid out of the roots."

Sheerah decided to take her frustrations out on the roots in the wooden tray. She pounded and smashed the roots with all her might. When Naamah came back to check her progress, she was pleased to see that Sheerah had done quite a good job.

"This is how we take the root remains out of the mix and then combine the flour with the moisture you crushed from the roots." Naamah then showed her how to use the specially carved wooden scraper to mix the flour and root juice, adding water a little at a time to make a thick dough. There were many steps, and she hoped Sheerah would eventually make wonderful bread on her own.

"Why did you take dough out of the mixing tray and put it into this other one?" Sheerah asked.

"I'll show you," Naamah said, pleased that Sheerah was at last showing some interest in the process. Half of the dough was mixed with mashed-up dates and covered with a cloth. "See?" she said as she moved. "The fruit causes the dough to get bigger and the bread to be taller," she explained.

The remaining part of the dough was pushed and pulled in the mixing tray with just a little olive oil until it was quite stretchy. Naamah showed Sheerah how to stretch the dough and shape it. While Sheerah finished, Naamah went to check the oven. *Seems about right,* she thought. *I would like Sheerah's first attempt at making bread to be somewhat successful.* Looking doubtful, Sheerah grabbed her oval-shaped dough and carried it towards Naamah and the oven.

"Careful there, don't let go of the cloth and drop the dough."

Naamah picked up an oval in each hand and, one after the other, stuck them to the sidewalls of the oven. She was reluctant to have Sheerah put her hands into the oven, but she had to learn, and Naamah had left several easily reached spots open for her.

"Ouch!" Sheerah said, pulling her hand away from the heat.

"It's not too bad once you get used to it," Naamah told her. Sheerah tried again but ended up dropping the bread onto the dung fire. She managed to get one oval to stick to the oven wall, and that buoyed her confidence. Soon enough, the rest of the ovals were baking.

"Let's check our other batch," Naamah said, as she saw Sheerah's interest begin to fade.

"Okay, Naamah," came the slightly weary reply.

They peeked under the cloth over the other mixing tray. Sheerah was surprised to see that the dough was rising.

"How did it get bigger?" Sheerah inquired.

"The fruit makes it do that, but it is still not quite ready." Naamah sensed Sheerah was losing the little interest she had. Her charge needed a break. "Go," Naamah said. "Build for a while, and I will come get you when it's time to bake these loaves."

Sheerah took off like an arrow toward her play building area. Several hours later, Sheerah came looking for Naamah. "Is it ready yet?" she asked.

"Let's go take a look," said Naamah.

Sheerah was surprised to see the cloth sitting atop the mixing tray. Her eyes were almost bulging when she asked, "What happened?"

Naamah smiled, then said, "Remember how I told you the fruit makes the dough grow? The fruit produces something that makes it bigger and tastier, too. Let's put it on the rack in the oven." She showed Sheerah a rack made of small, green pieces of wood lashed into a lattice with wet leather strips. She pointed to it and showed Sheerah, "This rack keeps the bread off the dung fire but doesn't burn itself."

Sheerah inhaled the air with obvious pleasure as the date bread baked. "That smells so good," she said.

CHAPTER TEN

S HEERAH WOKE UP. *It is still dark. Why am I awake?* she wondered. Then she remembered the dream and smiled. *The boy with the horses; why was he in my dream? It was fun walking together in that green field. Where was that? Abba had talked about such places, very far away. I will ask Naamah.* She went back to sleep with a smile on her face.

A little while later, after the sun came up and Naamah was calling her for breakfast, Sheerah's eyes shot open with excitement for the new day. Instead of curling up in her blankets, as she usually did, she jumped up. The dream was still vivid, and she wanted to ask Naamah about it. When she found her, words practically leapt out of her mouth. "Naamah, I have a question."

"What is it, dear one?"

"I had a dream last night. It was strange."

Naamah's ears perked up a bit. "What was the dream about?"

Sheerah felt unaccountably shy now that they were talking about it. "Well…it was about green fields. Are green fields real?"

"Yes, they are real," Naamah said. *That is the territory where*

Abigail's home was, she remembered suddenly. "What else happened in the dream?" she inquired.

Sheerah looked at the ground and traced some lines on the tile with her toe. "Well..." she said, starting with hesitation. "Do you remember the boy with the horses, Zeruiah? Well, he was in the dream," she finished in a rush.

Naamah smiled. "That's interesting," she said. "Finish your breakfast, and I will be right back. I need to talk to your Abba and Eema for a minute."

Naamah hurried to Ephraim's house. She curtsied low in the doorway, requesting entrance. Shuai happened to be there, and they were deep in conversation. Shuai noticed her first and motioned her into the room. Naamah came in and curtsied again.

"Hello, Naamah," Shuai said as Ephraim nodded.

"I came to tell you about a dream your daughter related to me this morning."

"A child's dream? Why?" Ephraim asked.

"It's the content of the dream that was striking. Sheerah talked about green fields, which she had never seen. But she also mentioned Zeruiah.

Ephraim and Shuai gave one another a brief look, then Ephraim began to smile. "It's time to tell her, you know," he said to his wife.

"I know you are right, my husband, but she is only nine. She's not yet ten years old."

"Yes, she is nine," he said. And if I understand correctly, she is woefully behind in learning to manage a household."

Shuai started to say, "Her bread making has really improved and—" One look at Ephraim's face told her he was right. "Naamah," she turned and said, "please teach her all she needs to know. No more playing in the dirt, building her towns."

"Yes, ma'am," Naamah replied. "I will accelerate her progress. Her wedding is only three years away."

Something like a cloud passed briefly across Shuai's face. "Only three years," she repeated.

"Naamah, please bring Sheerah to see us," Ephraim said.

Naamah hurried back to Sheerah and ran into her as she was walking. "I asked you to wait for me," she said crossly.

Sheerah bowed her head, whispering, "I was tired of waiting."

The nursemaid tried to be stern with Sheerah, but couldn't manage it. She only said, "You need to go see your Eema and Abba." And then she started walking. Sheerah ran ahead of her to her father's house and went directly up to her Abba for a hug. He readily obliged, then released her to hug her mother, then they all sat on the rug.

"How old are you, Sheerah?" Ephraim asked.

"Almost ten," she said happily. "My birthday is in a few months."

"Have you thought about marriage?" he inquired.

Sheerah looked shocked, then afraid. She thought, *I have to marry? Whom? Surely not the old man who visited recently.* She answered slowly, looking at the colorful rug around her. "No," she said. Then she thought of the dream. *Maybe I could marry Zeruiah. That wouldn't be so bad since he is about my age.*

Shuai was speaking to her. She looked up at her mother. What did she say? She was talking about the caravan. *Of course,* she thought, *I remember the caravan. That's where I met Zeruiah.*

"Yes, I remember," she said to her mother.

"Your Abba and I spoke to Abigail when the caravan was here. She suggested we join our families with a marriage between you and her son, Zeruiah. Shuai searched her daughter's face for some sign of acceptance, but what she saw was a slow, shy smile come across her face. "Would that be acceptable to you? It would not be for three more years." Her daughter's eyes seemed lit from within.

Sheerah knew her mother was just being kind. She knew a

deal had already been made for her future, and it would benefit both families. *I am so grateful that he is the groom they have chosen for me,* Sheerah thought. *But having babies and running a household, how will I be able to do it?*

Shuai was waiting for an answer. "Naamah would, of course, be going with you when the time comes."

At hearing that, Sheerah's shoulders sagged with relief. She felt more grown-up already. *So much to think about.* She thanked her parents for their considerate choice. Then she kissed each one on the cheek and left.

Naamah was waiting just outside the doorway. She overheard everything being said. When Sheerah came out, she looked at her nurse with large eyes. Naamah said, "We'd better get busy; there is a lot to learn."

Sheerah nodded dreamily.

Naamah continued, "You will probably have servants for much of your household work, but you need to know how to do everything you expect them to do so you can guide them."

Sheerah had trouble focusing on anything but what her parents had just told her. *What was Naamah saying?* Once again, she pulled her focus back. "OK, where do we start?"

"We've already started. Your bread-making skills are getting better every day."

"So that is what that was all about!"

CHAPTER ELEVEN

"WHAT ARE WE going to do today?" Sheerah was not at all tired from yesterday's exertions.

"Today we are going to learn about making cloth for clothing and blankets."

Sheerah looked quizzically at Naamah.

Naamah chuckled at Sheerah's confusion. "Did you think your tunics and bedcovers just appeared?"

"I never thought about it."

"That's all right. You'll learn about it over the next few days."

Sheerah seemed to gather her courage as she sighed, "Let's get started." And they started with fervor. The two spent the morning talking about fabric making.

"What are these weeds for? How are they going to make soft cloth?"

Naamah replied, "These are not weeds; they are flax, which is carefully grown. Several of the servants are working with it now. See how they pull the plants up by the roots? They are tied up and left to dry." Naamah pointed to her right. "Another servant is breaking some older flax over a board and scraping it with a wooden blade. See how the fibers are starting to line up?"

"When do *we* do something?" Sheerah asked, becoming impatient.

"You'll get your turn very soon," Naamah said with a small smile. She walked to one of the servants and asked if there was any flax ready for the next step. He indicated a small stack and gave her the rake-like object. Sheerah looked at it, mystified.

"Now, dear one, we will clean the beaten flax by pulling each bunch through the tines." Naamah repeatedly pulled the flax through the tines on the rake, and Sheerah could see that the fibers were lining up. The seeds fell into the cloth at their feet. "Why are you doing that?" Sheerah asked.

"Those seeds are for next year's crop," she told Sheerah. "Be careful not to lose any."

"Okay." *Good thing I didn't shake the cloth to get the dirt off.*

Naamah showed her the hair-like fibers that had become visible. Then she gathered and combed them into a small pile.

"This still doesn't look like cloth," Sheerah noted.

"Be patient," replied Naamah. "We still have a long way to go before we make you a new tunic."

Sheerah made an effort to calm her impatience. "Okay, what is next?"

"We will spin the fibers into thread, like this." Naamah expertly balanced a weighted stick on her thigh. Taking a few strands of the delicate flax fiber, she wet them so they would stick together. Each strand was then attached to the spindle, and Naamah spun the stick while pulling the fiber to create a thread. The smooth, almost effortless rhythm of Naamah's spinning was the result of many years of practice. Sheerah became fascinated by the repetitive activity and was surprised when Naamah said it was her turn.

"Next, we will wind the thread I made on a shuttle for the weaving process we will do later."

Sheerah didn't expect to do the spinning as well as Naamah,

but she had no idea what a disaster it would be. Naamah gave her only a very small bunch to start so as not to waste the precious flax.

For Sheerah, the fiber fell off the spindle before she could even try to start spinning. When she did get to the spinning process, the spindle tumbled out of her grasp and fell on the ground. Naamah was aching to take the spindle from her and ease her frustration and tears, but she knew she must let Sheerah keep trying so she could master it. Finally, Naamah could stand it no longer and said, "Go do some building, I'll finish this up."

Sheerah had never looked so grateful as she ran off.

She must learn somehow, Naamah thought to herself.

CHAPTER TWELVE

THE NEXT DAY dawned clear and hot. Sheerah didn't want more household lessons but knew that Naamah would insist. *I don't want to spin anymore,* Sheerah thought. *Naamah did mention weaving yesterday. Maybe that would be easier to master.*

Naamah brought breakfast, and Sheerah knew there would be no more stalling once it was finished. She ate slowly, but eventually she had no more ability to delay, and Naamah led Sheerah to the area they had used yesterday for spinning. She looked warily at the contraption the servants had leaned against the house. "What is this?" Sheerah asked as she gazed at the wooden frame and the multitude of strings with small clay balls dangling from each one.

"This is a loom, and a very fine one, dear Sheerah."

The frame was a wooden rectangle, with a horizontal piece of wood that had been lashed to the frame mid-way up. At the base of the frame were strings, draping from back to front and over the top. The strings had clay weights to keep them pulled taut. Some weights were placed in front of the horizontal piece alternating in front and behind the bar.

Oh my, this looks decidedly more complicated than the spinning I attempted yesterday. She wondered. *Will I ever be able to run a household of my own?* She started to despair and then heard Naamah.

What was Naamah saying?

"...the threads running in the long direction on the loom are called the warp. The clay weights suspend the threads vertically and keep them straight." Naamah showed her the shuttle made of polished wood with spun thread wrapped around it.

Sheerah turned the shuttle over and over in her hands. It had a dull point on each end and was about five inches long. The wood was as smooth as some of the pillows in Abigail's tent.

"Why is it so smooth?" Sheerah asked Naamah.

"We don't want the spun thread to catch, because that might pull the delicate strands of the thread apart. Now, let me show you what you will do."

Naamah positioned herself in front of the loom on a small stool. She pushed the shuttle in between the warp threads all the way across the loom. With a very large wooden comb, she pushed the new weft threads down into the weaving already on the loom. After she finished pushing, Naamah brought the shuttle back to where it started, and another row was finished and combed into place.

That looks easy enough, Sheerah considered. "Let me try!"

Naamah was pleased at her enthusiasm and showed her where to sit so her hands would reach the work. She handed Sheerah the shuttle, which Sheerah promptly dropped in the dirt.

"Try again, little one," Naamah said. "You will get better the more you try."

Sheerah tried to concentrate on the process. She was able to get the shuttle across once, but on its trip back, one of the children called her name. She turned to berate the interloper, lost her focus, and managed to get the shuttle tangled in the warp threads. Naamah was quick to help, but the tangle was hopeless. There was no remedy for the situation but to cut the threads, leaving a remnant of ruined fabric behind.

"So now you get to see how to string a loom," Naamah said.

"I'm truly sorry, Naamah. I was so frustrated." *I hope Naamah will have pity on me and allow me to go play, thus rescuing me from the loom mess* Sheerah thought. But she saw the determined look on her nurse's face. *No way, she wants me to fix it. This is hopeless!*

"Start by cutting the weights off each string and placing them in a row," Naamah instructed. "Put them here on the shelf so we can see how many we have."

Sheerah started the easy task, wondering how in the world this mess would ever become a loom again.

Naamah was soothing as she taught. "The strings are too valuable to discard; we will stretch them out on the ground."

Untangling as she went, Naamah was able to salvage all but a few short pieces, which had become too knotted to reuse. Sheerah was impressed. Starting at the edge where the trouble started, Naamah stretched the thread on the loom and said, "Here now, Sheerah. As I go, tie a weight on each string so it is held firm and kept vertical."

Between the two of them, the loom was repaired.

With more practice, Sheerah was eventually able to weave a passable piece of fabric. Soon after, she felt a little more confident, she and Naamah made a pillow from it for Sheerah's bed.

CHAPTER THIRTEEN

S HEERAH STRETCHED LAZILY in bed on a beautiful morning when she was twelve years old. Suddenly, she noticed a wetness on her lady parts. *Did I wet my bed? I have not done that for as long as I can remember.* She could hear Naamah rising for the day. *Oh no,* she thought, *how will I ever explain this? I'd better take a look.* As she did, she felt a scream rise from her throat. The wetness was blood! *I wasn't hurt anywhere. Why is there blood on my bedclothes?* She stood up, and her sleeping tunic was bloody too. Just then, Naamah swept into the room. She took in the sight and then smiled very big. *What is she smiling about? I may be dying here. How sad to die at twelve years of age.*

Naamah noticed Sheerah's look of dismay. Shuai was supposed to talk to her about this. *Either Sheerah wasn't listening, or Shuai got busy and forgot. Now the task falls to me,* thought Naamah. First, she needed to comfort the scared child. She could talk to her while they cleaned up.

"Sheerah, this is a happy day!"

"It is?" Sheerah said, eyes brimming with tears. "How so?"

"Your moon time," began Naamah, "shows that you are a woman now. Stay here, and I will get some supplies."

"Don't go!"

"I'm only going to my sleeping chamber. I'll be right back, I promise." Naamah went to her room and retrieved some strips of soft wool and an undergarment wrap. When Naamah returned to Sheerah's room, she found her crying, curled up in a corner. When she walked up to her, Sheerah went from scared to angry.

"Are you excited that I am dying?" Sheerah asked with some petulance.

"No, no, you are not dying, dear one. This happens to virtually every woman." Naamah assured her.

"I've never heard about it, even from my cousins."

"It isn't something that is discussed except between the woman and her mother or nursemaid, and never before men."

"Have you ever noticed that sometimes, lots of the women are 'missing' from activities?"

Sheerah shook her head.

"Well, it happens almost every month. When it does, you will find them in the little tent at the base of the hill. No one goes down there except women in their moon time and those few who bring them food and water. In a couple of weeks, the ladies currently in the little round tent would return the favor."

"I, I didn't know..." Sheerah said, bewildered. Naamah wanted to hold her little one, but she was on her moon time. "Let's get you cleaned up, and I'll show you the way."

Later, wearing a new tunic and a wad of lamb's wool in her undergarment wrap, Sheerah and Naamah set off. Before they were even close, they heard peals of laughter coming from the little round tent. Sheerah looked at Naamah in surprise.

"Not so bad after all, is it, little one?" Naamah thought as she spoke, *I will have to stop calling her that now.*

As her countenance became brighter, Sheerah's apprehension seemed to lift. They arrived at the tent and stepped inside. It was cozy, with pillows and mats. Some of the ladies seemed a little surprised to see Sheerah, but everyone made her feel welcome.

Moments after their arrival, Shuai entered the tent, breathless. "I'm so sorry I didn't prepare you for this, Sheerah! I can't believe the time has gone by so fast. It seems like you were just a baby a moment ago." Shuai smiled with tears in her eyes. She patted Sheerah's hand and led her over to an area where they could rest. "Let's talk about your wedding!"

When the ladies heard that, the chatting and giggling began anew. This was the only time the women had to themselves, and they took advantage of it. Just then, friends arrived with their supper.

CHAPTER FOURTEEN

S HEERAH FINISHED CHANGING her tunic. She never failed to make a mess of her clothes while making bread, but it was now in the oven and smelling delicious. She was about to put on her second shoe when there was a commotion downstairs. *What was going on near the front door?* she wondered.

She heard Shuai and Naamah laughing in a peculiar tone. Even more mystified, Sheerah came down the steps trying in vain to see around the corner. She arrived at the front door and was shocked to see who the visitor was.

Zeruiah was standing in the doorway with a big grin on his face.

Although she still thought of him as "the boy with the horses," which was how he appeared in occasional dreams, he was now a young man. He even had facial hair! Sheerah was flabbergasted and couldn't move.

"Say hello to Zeruiah, Sheerah!" Shuai urgently said to her.

Sheerah felt rooted to the ground and was as silent as the cedar trees outside. Her discomfiture was interrupted by the arrival of her Abba, who had a big grin on his face. He heartily embraced Zeruiah in greeting. This seemed to eliminate Sheerah's "spell" of stillness, and she smiled broadly at her visitor.

"Hello, Zeruiah," Sheerah said. "I'm pleasantly surprised to see you. What brings you to our home?"

"Well," he said. Apparently, it was his turn to be shy. "I...I came to see you."

"Oh, my," she said. Sheerah couldn't think of anything else to say.

"Even though our wedding is not until next year, I brought you a wedding present," Zeruiah explained.

Was it coming up so soon? What kind of present? Sheerah wondered. Zeruiah turned back to the entrance and whistled, and Sheerah was startled to see a horse come trotting up to Zeruiah. The horse nuzzled his robes, and Zeruiah laughed. It was clearly looking for treats.

Turning back to Sheerah, he said, "This is my gift to you. She is very well-trained, and your servants can talk to mine about her care."

A horse, a horse of my very own. I can't believe it! She marveled. She looked at Abba, expecting to see a scowl and a head shaking, indicating she couldn't have the gift. Instead, she saw him smile indulgently at her and then at Zeruiah. Sheerah had no idea that a horse had been part of the bride-price negotiations. Though they settled on something else, Abigail and Zeruiah had decided to give one to her anyway.

"It is a very handsome gift. Thank you, and thank your mother for me," Ephraim spoke at last.

"Sheerah, would you take a walk with me?" Zeruiah inquired. He looked at Ephraim as if asking permission. Ephraim nodded and looked at Naamah, who smiled and gathered her shawl about her to join them.

"Yes, I'd like that, and Naamah will accompany us. "

Zeruiah smiled, took the reins of the horse, and started towards the yard with Sheerah. Naamah followed behind at a close but respectable pace. Once out of the immediate view of the front door, Zeruiah looked back and motioned for Sheerah to walk alongside him.

"What is the horse's name?" Sheerah inquired.

"Name?" Zeruiah said, looking baffled. He had lots of horses but hadn't given any of them proper names.

Well, I can't just call her "Horse," can I?

"What name would you give her?" he replied. "She's yours."

"I'll call her Butter since she is the color of butter."

"Very well, Butter it is."

They both fell silent but could hear Naamah snickering behind them.

Giving an animal a name! Naamah thought. *Leave it to Sheerah.*

Sheerah and Zeruiah spoke very little as they walked. But Sheerah was struck by Zeruiah's warmth and kindness. *Maybe being married wouldn't be so bad after all,* she thought. Just as they approached her home, before Naamah could intervene, Zeruiah impulsively grabbed Sheerah's hand and kissed her fingertips. She blushed and looked intently at Butter.

Naamah rushed to the two, stepped in between them, and said, "Thank you for visiting Master Zeruiah. Sheerah, come with me, please."

"What about Butter?" Sheerah inquired with worry in her voice.

"The servants will see to the horse. But you need to come with me now!"

"Good-bye, Zeruiah," Sheerah managed to shout over her shoulder as Naamah dragged her toward the house.

"You are the daughter of a great leader. You cannot be seen dallying around with anyone, even the one you are going to marry," Naamah scolded.

Sheerah was so caught up with Zeruiah and Butter, the horse, she hardly heard anything Naamah had to say. Naamah was still talking as they went inside.

What a wonderful day! Sheerah mused, barely aware.

CHAPTER FIFTEEN

SHUAI CAME INTO Sheerah's room early with great excitement. Preparations for Sheerah's wedding clothing were well underway. Today, she wanted Sheerah to try on the clothing that had been made for the occasion. She hoped her daughter would like the tunics, wraps, skirts, and assorted accessories. Sheerah was still waking up as Shuai spread the three new tunics out on the end of Sheerah's bed. When she was fully awake, Sheerah gasped at the beauty before her.

The extravagance of three new tunics at once made her speechless. They were all different, but each one had been decorated with shells that were dyed in colors derived from fruits and vegetables. One tunic had buttons carved from bone running down the front. Her favorite, though, was the one with tiny shells embroidered around the neck. They were dark pink, and she thought the design came from a dressmaker's dream.

"I think this one with the pink shells would be good for the wedding," Sheerah said.

"Don't forget, Abigail will have made some things for her new daughter-in-law as well. You must not offend her by choosing something else for the actual wedding ceremony. In the days following the ceremony, you can wear whatever you like," Shuai responded. "But for the wedding ceremony, defer to her as a sign of respect."

Sheerah turned to the next pile and began looking through the jewelry next to the tunics. A few things she recognized from the caravan that had come several years ago. Her Eema was already thinking about Sheerah's wedding, all those years ago, and it was yet more proof of her love. The thought brought tears to her eyes. Suddenly, Sheerah noticed something shiny. She located the shiny object; it was a circle of bronze with crossed bars in the center. *What could this be for?* Sheerah thought. *It's so beautiful, and bronze is so valuable.*

Shuai noticed her consternation and said, "This is a holder for your shawl or a belt. You pass the material through one side and into the other side, then give it a tug, and it will hold. Let me show you."

Shuai expertly pushed the fabric of her shawl through one of the openings and then pushed it back down through the opposite one. She showed Sheerah how to tug on the fabric of the shawl, adjusting it so it didn't slip off her shoulders. "Now, you try it" she said, handing the holder to Sheerah. "More than likely, Abigail will have a lovely shawl for you to wear for the wedding ceremony. This ring will hold it in place nicely."

Sheerah gulped to hold back her tears. Her Eema thought of everything. Sheerah stepped close and gave her mother a big hug.

"I will miss you so much, Eema."

At that, they both began to cry. It was likely that they might not see each other again after the wedding.

Their sadness was interrupted by the announcement that Zeruiah was visiting again.

Chapter Sixteen

ESPITE EVERYTHING, SHEERAH felt happy to learn her betrothed was visiting again, and she raced down the steps to greet him. Naamah was waiting for her and said, "Tie this shawl around your waist."

What was Naamah fussing about? Sheerah impatiently asked, "Why?"

"You need to be modest!" Naamah said sharply. "You are not a child anymore. Wait for me to accompany you."

Sheerah reluctantly stopped and tied the large shawl around her waist. Naamah stayed close behind as she continued down the steps. She stopped shyly just before the doorway.

There he was, waiting for her at the entrance.

"Hello, Zeruiah," she said with her eyes shyly looking at his feet.

He seemed excited to see her, and he had Butter with him. The horse was wearing a blanket with straps hanging down on either side of her belly. *Was he taking his gift back?* She worried.

"Sheerah," he said, full of calm excitement, "can you come with me, please?"

Zeruiah led her and Butter over to a large rock in the yard. "You're going to learn to ride today." Naamah looked dubious, but she stayed close.

Zeruiah assisted Sheerah as she climbed up on the rock while Naamah watched dubiously. Once she was atop the rock, Zeruiah moved Butter closer and told her to throw her leg over Butter's back.

I'm really not sure about this, Sheerah thought, *it's a long way down from here!* But she did as he requested and landed securely, but it didn't make her completely confident. Zeruiah seemed to take his time and be patient with her as she found her confidence. Once Sheerah was seated on the horse, her betrothed gently took her foot and placed it in the strap on the near side of the horse. He went around and did the same with her other foot. She felt glad of her modest shawl now. From the ground, he showed her the horse's mane and made her hang on to the hair when she needed to. Sheerah's heart began racing as she sat on Butter.

Zeruiah left her side and went to Butter's head. Still amused that a horse had a name, he picked up the reins.

Uh-oh, Butter is moving, she thought. *It's OK. Much easier to ride than a camel.* After a few minutes, she felt sure of herself and changed her mind. *This is fun,* she thought, *I like this a lot.*

Zeruiah scanned Sheerah's face repeatedly, and when she noticed, she realized she had been frowning with concentration. She deliberately smiled as broad a smile as she could.

"This is wonderful!" she said, full of enthusiasm.

When he heard her excitement, Zeruiah relaxed. "I was worried for a moment," he said.

He walked the horse a little faster, making sure Sheerah held on to Butter's mane. "You're a natural," he said to Sheerah as he moved even more quickly. They began circling the yard and came up past the front door again. Naamah struggled to keep up with them.

Suddenly, Butter stopped.

Sheerah heard a squishy, plopping sound. Once Butter was done, Zeruiah called out, "Where is your dung heap?" Sheerah pointed to an area not too far from the bread-baking oven. Zeruiah dropped the reins to the ground and strode across the yard, returning with the dung shovel.

Sheerah was amazed. Butter didn't move at all while Zeruiah went to fetch the shovel. He cleaned up and walked away again, leaving the manure on the fresh side of the dung heap. Closer to the oven, the dung used for fuel had already dried. It would not be so pungent when used for bread baking.

Butter stood, almost bored.

Zeruiah returned, and the lesson continued. He placed the reins on either side of the horse's head and handed them to Sheerah. *Wait,* Sheerah thought with alarm. *I can't hold the mane and the reins too.*

"Hold the reins in one hand, " Zeruiah told her, "but not too tightly. Then, you can still hold the mane if you need to. Sheerah remained amazed at how calm Zeruiah was while he taught her. He was very patient and held Butter's head while she adjusted to this new situation.

After a pause, Zeruiah let go and started walking away. Butter followed him. In response, Sheerah accidentally pulled the reins against Butter's neck. When she did that, Butter turned and started walking to the left. Zeruiah smiled to himself. He walked over to Butter and made the horse stop.

"If you want her to turn," he said, "lay the reins on her neck like you just did. To turn her the other direction, lay the reins on the other side of her neck. If you want her to stop, pull back on the reins."

Amazing; I am actually riding a horse! Sheerah exulted in her mind.

Naamah's chaperoning duties were wearing her out, and she was glad when Zeriuah slowed the horse's pace. But it was still a long visit.

CHAPTER SEVENTEEN

ALL TOO SOON, it was time for Zeruiah to leave. He showed her how to wipe Butter down before the servants took the horse for further care. Sheerah took to it with enthusiasm and talked soothingly to the horse.

Then it was time for Zeruiah to leave. He waved as he departed, crushing Sheerah's heart more than she was expecting. She knew she would miss Zeruiah after this visit. And the wedding was still nine months away.

She and Naamah returned to the house. Naamah fanned herself. "Did you see, Naamah?" she asked. "You saw me! I was riding!"

"Yes," Naamah replied. "And I think it is dangerous."

"Oh no," Sheerah blurted. "Butter is very gentle! And with the straps for my feet and the mane to hold onto, I felt very secure up there."

"Well, that's fine," Naamah informed her, "but we have more work to do." We need to work on your frontlets. They won't bead themselves; you know."

Much to Naamah's surprise, Sheerah agreed. "Let's get started," Sheerah said with enthusiasm.

They cleaned up and then headed to where her mother sat, waiting. Shuai had made one frontlet for Sheerah. It was similar to the decorative headband resting on Sheerah's forehead. The one Shuai had just made was covered with beautiful shells and stones and had an attached ornament, a bright blue gem, right in the center. Sheerah recognized it immediately as the lapis lazuli from the caravan that she had given to Eema. Sheerah knew her Eema loved that piece, but now it was a part of her own wedding clothes. *My mind is made up,* Sheerah thought fondly. *Regardless of what her new mother-in-law made for me, this is going to be on my forehead for the wedding. I hope Zeruiah likes it.*

Naamah showed her the slender bone needle she would use, with its hook to hold the fiber, and make clothes. Shuai and Naamah were careful teachers, and Sheerah paid close attention while they showed her how to do things.

Sheerah's fingers tingled as she watched Naamah push the needle partway through the soft leather, then hook the fiber thread and pull it through. "Now we add an ornament and push the needle back through the leather," Naamah explained. "Snug the ornament down tight and repeat the whole process."

It must have taken Shuai forever to create all the tunics, decorations, and that amazing frontlet, Sheerah thought. *How can I ever thank her?* She felt a little tear in the corner of her eye. *I must tell her today how much I appreciate all she has done.* And then she began to try her hand at sewing a frontlet.

"This is hard," Sheerah said. Naamah corrected her technique slightly, and it became a little easier to do. Sheerah kept at her work while Naamah stepped out to start preparing the next meal.

Her frontlet was looking prettier with every ornament she added. *I can do this!* she thought, smiling to herself. *Maybe I'll make more.* Just then, Naamah came into the room where Sheerah was working, her arms full of bed linens.

Sheerah thought, *Now what?*

"What are those for?" she inquired.

"You must have more than clothing to go to your marriage," said Naamah. "We are going to make bedsheets. They will be extra nice. Sheerah stopped what she was doing and walked over to touch the linens.

"These are so soft!" Sheerah exclaimed.

Naamah looked pleased. "They were given extra washings on the rocks and stomped on by the servants as a gift for your wedding."

Sheerah had never felt anything so soft. "What could we possibly do to make them nicer?"

"We will be embroidering them."

"Embroidering?"

"Sewing threads through the cloth in decorative patterns."

Now, this was interesting to Sheerah. She had been putting decorations on her buildings of late. "Like I put on my buildings?"

Naamah said, "Some of those decorations might be nice. And how about some flowers and pomegranates?"

"Okay," Sheerah said, excitement finally showing. "This is much more interesting than making bread and spinning and weaving."

Sheerah's creativity had been ignited, and she would later look back on this day as the beginning of her building career for real.

CHAPTER EIGHTEEN

T WO WEEKS AWAY. *The wedding was only two weeks away. How is that possible?* Sheerah mused. All the preparations had kept her so busy, but everything was now in order.

Ephraim had been readying the household to travel to Abigail's home for the last month. The dowry was complete and set apart for travel. Sheerah was the most excited he'd seen her in weeks.

Such a momentous occasion, he thought. His favorite daughter was getting married, and they made a covenant with Abigail to join their lands. They would each be gaining a substantial area of territory.

Butter required extra preparation for feeding and care, but Sheerah refused to leave her behind. There would be objections, of course, but her mind was made up. She wanted to ride Butter into the wedding ceremony for her grand entrance. Sheerah could almost hear Naamah's comments, *"It is not done. No one would do that. Everyone would be astonished."* Sheerah giggled to herself.

She was truly only interested in the look on Zeruiah's face as she rode in unassisted on the horse he had given her. She had been practicing as much as she could, and she felt amazingly comfortable on Butter. Ephraim balked at the idea of letting her ride to Abigail's on the horse when she asked him. "Too dangerous," he kept saying. *Both from the aspect of my personal safety and the covenant to be made with Abigail,* Sheerah thought. She appreciated his care, despite his answer. But she was going to ride to Zeruiah on her wedding day.

I'm really going to miss my family and my home, Sheerah thought tearfully. Perhaps she and Zeruiah could visit her home after they were married. *The journey was long, but Zeruiah came to visit her and brought Butter. So maybe...*

That night, Sheerah had a dream. It was a disturbing one, so she told Naamah about it.

"It was very happy with Zeruiah," she began, "and we had two babies in the dream. But suddenly, black clouds gathered on the horizon and began moving toward us. I gathered up the babies and turned to find Zeruiah, but he was nowhere to be seen. What could this mean?"

Naamah looked troubled. She said, "I don't know the meanings of dreams. How could I?" Thinking to herself, Naamah mused, *What could it mean? It did not sound good. And anyway, we need to finish packing these boxes of Sheerah's things. I am so glad to be going with her. Separating from her would break my heart.*

Naamah returned to sorting and packing. "Sheerah, do you want to take this?" Naamah said, holding up a small carving of a wooden camel.

"No. Now that I have Butter, I don't care about camels anymore."

"Does your Eema know you are wearing your wedding jewelry around the house?"

"Probably not," Sheerah sighed, and handed the jewelry to Naamah. "It is so pretty! I cannot wait to wear it." Naamah carefully packed it away between layers of linen. "This box is done. The servants will be along shortly to get your boxes for loading. Do not remove anything from any of the boxes. They all need to go to our new home."

Sheerah had tears in her eyes again. "I can never thank you enough for going with me."

Naamah saw no reason to tell her that her services were part of the marriage covenant. She gave Sheerah a big hug, kissed her on the cheek.

"Don't cry now," said Naamah. "There will be time enough for that. We leave tomorrow for a week's hard travel."

Chapter Nineteen

T HE SUN WAS red in the exceedingly early sunrise, but the household was already awake and bustling about getting ready to leave. The entire household would be going along to serve the family on the way. Ephraim was leaving a small group of servants to protect the property, but everyone else was coming.

Sheerah was up and sitting on her bed for the last time. *I'm not sure whether to be happy or sad,* she thought. *I am looking forward to seeing Zeruiah again, but what if he is displeased with me? I have heard stories of men displeased with their wives on the wedding night, casting them out into the desert where they would die. Zeruiah would not do such a thing, would he? I must be pleasing to him in every way. I think that is what I want anyway.*

Shuai came looking for Sheerah with last-minute instructions for her daughter, which needed to be shared before they started traveling and had no privacy.

"My dear girl, how I will miss you," she said when she saw her daughter. "It will break my heart, but it will help when I know that you are safe and getting along well with your new family. Remember, Zeruiah is your lord once you are married. Do not contradict him in anything, especially if there is anyone else present. Keep yourself as clean as you are able and use this occasionally." She handed Sheerah a small vial of perfume. Tears ran down the cheeks of both mother and daughter.

"Thank you, Eema. You think of everything. I will always love you."

They took a moment to embrace and share beautiful tears. But then it was time to go. Before long, the household procession started off. Male servants and Ephraim walked in front, the women in the middle, and the shepherds brought up the rear. Their flocks and herds for the journey and for the dowry followed behind them in relatively tight organization. The procession was extensive, and the tinkling of the bells on the goats rang out. Since the flocks were at the very back, their smell (and the manure) was not a problem for the rest of the entourage. It was a long day's journey to the first oasis and would be dark by the time they arrived.

The day dragged on with a sweltering heaviness. Even though summer was waning, it was still very hot. *And I'm riding this stinky camel and not even walking like the Naamah and the others are doing.* Sheerah found herself feeling empathy for the servants and herdsmen. *I wonder why that never occurred to me before.* She resolved to treat any servants she was in contact with in a gentle way.

Finally, the guiding servants from Abigail's household called out. They had spotted the oasis. It was so late that the servants threw down blankets willy-nilly for the various groups. Sheerah was so anxious to get down from her camel and check on Butter, but she had to wait. The servants prevented her from going amongst the herdsmen and shepherds, assuring her that they would carefully tend to her horse's needs.

People were tired and ready to go to sleep, but while the night grew darker, people passed dates and bread around for supper. The stars began twinkling overhead in the cooling of the night. Except for the usual animal sounds everyone was accustomed to, the encampment became quiet.

In the middle of the night, Sheerah was awakened simultaneously by shouts, cries, and screams. There was intense stinging and itching on her legs, arms, and even her face. She jumped up and began brushing off her skin as much as she could.

There were fire ants everywhere.

Everyone in the camp began jumping and flailing about. They must have disturbed several nests upon arrival. The only people unaffected were the shepherds and herdsmen who, covered in a coating of dirt, were protected.

This itching is maddening. I wish I were back on my camel now, Sheerah thought as she tried to scratch her whole body at once. She reached to scratch her face and her arm was grabbed by Naamah.

"Do not mar your face," she snapped. "The wedding is in less than a week." Naamah tried to apologize with a gentler touch. Sheerah understood and squeezed her hand gently.

This was a terrible night for everyone.

Servants lit torches, scouring the area for an unaffected piece of ground where the family could sit. There would be no more sleep tonight. Naamah went away for a moment, then returned to Sheerah's side with some ointment. She insisted that Sheerah put it on her face. It smelled horrible, but it did quell the itching a bit.

How would I make it without Naamah? Sheerah thought, overcome with gratitude.

Daylight finally arrived, and the extent of the damage was assessed. Many people in their company had angry, red spots and some welts from the fire ant attack. Sheerah saw everyone scratching, and some were cursing. *What a miserable start to the long-awaited trip,* she thought. The camp seemed to erupt with snapping noises as the servants attempted to rid the blankets of the pests, and she heard the occasional yell when a live one found its target on someone's skin.

She felt for her travel party.

Naamah kept peering intently at Sheerah's face. "Not too bad, but you must not scratch. That spreads the fire ant's poison," Naamah warned. "I want you to be your beautiful self for your groom. Put on more ointment."

"It stinks so much," Sheerah replied, "but it seems to be working. Is Butter all right?"

"Check on her if you must," her nurse replied. "But be careful where you step. The ointment will protect a little bit, but you can still get stung."

That was all Sheerah needed to hear before she rushed to find her horse. Butter was fine, and Sheerah could not detect any bites on her. She was so relieved.

Butter needed to be in prime condition for the wedding.

CHAPTER TWENTY

Z ERUIAH NEARLY SHOUTED at his mother as he firmly
said, "I am a man, and I am going to meet Sheerah
and her family."

"It just is not done, Zeruiah," his mother said, trying to convince
him of the severity of the situation. "How can I convince you
not to do this? It is dangerous to be alone in the area they are
passing through."

"I will take my servants and my personal guard, but I am
going!" He set his jaw and stared at his mother. She nodded
almost imperceptibly. *As he said,* she thought, *he is a grown
man.*

Barely out of sight of Abigail's territory, Zeruiah heard the
high-pitched, "yip, yip, ee-ah" meant to imitate the sound of
coyotes. It was clearly human in origin. *Bandits! Already?* he
thought. *I must protect Sheerah and her family!*

He yelled a quick command to his guards and servants
to come to his aid, but they were already surrounding him to
protect him. In mere moments, Zeruiah was in the center of a
circle of stalwart, loyal guards and servants.

The bandits appeared on the horizon.

Zeruiah counted five members in this group. His guards
brandished swords and spears. The captain of Zeruiah's guards

gave a loud shout, telling the bandits what would happen to them if they came any closer. Hearing the shouts, the bandits seemed to have thought better of attacking Zeruiah and his group because they slowed, turned around, and rode back toward the horizon.

Zeruiah's men cheered.

Now I am even more sure that I need to reach Sheerah's family to guard them from the bandits, Zeruiah thought. He and his cohorts gathered their belongings and hurried to intercept Sheerah and her family. Moving on horseback, Zeruiah and his guards and servants were covering the ground quickly. *Once we are married, I will improve this path between Ephraim's lands and ours,* he thought.

He did not find them right away, so his group was forced to make camp for the night. Plagued as he was with anxiety about Sheerah's safety, Zeruiah knew he would not be sleeping much. He was up and ready to travel at first light. The men didn't feel the urgency as keenly as he did and were slower to get organized for the day's travel than he wanted. Zeruiah got angry and yelled at the men, which encouraged them to get ready more quickly.

"I've never seen him like this," a servant said to one of the guards.

"Nor I," the guard replied.

"We had better move!" said the servant.

Zeruiah's company came to the crest of a hill. Below, he could see a camp in disarray. *Am I too late?* He thought. *Did the bandits already attack? What else could account for the blankets and camel saddles tossed about, seemingly at random.* His mind ran with fear.

Zeruiah rode down quickly, headed for the largest tent. *This should be Ephraim's.* He was relieved to see that Butter was securely tied outside. *No bandit would leave a horse behind. What happened?* He jumped down and ran unceremoniously through the doorway and into the tent. Inside, he found Sheerah, Naamah, Shuai, and Ephraim covered with red sting marks.

Fire ants!

What a relief! he thought. Joyous relief that it wasn't the bandits flooded his mind. *Not so for them. I must not laugh. They would not understand.*

Sheerah looked at him and lowered her eyes in embarrassment. He walked over to her and took her hand. "You are still beautiful, don't worry," Zeruiah said with calm reassurance. Her smile was cautious.

No wonder they were delayed. It will be a couple of days before the entourage can even try to move again. Zeruiah sent two servants back to inform Abigail that there would be a delay. *I'm sure they'll explain why with great detail.*

The rest of the trip was uneventful but slow. The caravan arrived at Abigail's luxurious home two days later, which was four days after their expected arrival.

Everyone, but especially Sheerah, was grateful to reach their destination.

CHAPTER TWENTY-ONE

S HEERAH WAS AWESTRUCK by the size and beauty of her new home when she arrived. It was tall, not unlike the typical two-story home. But where most homes had a flat roof, this one had a verdant garden on the roof of the second floor. She found out later that two servants were assigned the special and respected duty of hauling water to that garden and keeping the gardens lush. There were multiple chairs and other places to sit, and due to the plants, it was cool even in the heat of the desert day.

Abigail's welcoming servants were soon replaced by Abigail herself. Sheerah noticed that she smelled marvelous as a breeze brought her scent to the family. Her flowing silk clothing appeared comfortable and regal at the same time.

"Please come in and make yourselves comfortable," she said.

Shuai briefly embraced Abigail. She did it quickly and not too closely, since they were dirty from traveling. Abigail clapped her hands twice, and four new servants appeared. They were carrying towels draped over small earthenware pots of soap and perfume. Two of the servants went with Shuai, Sheerah, and Naamah at the indication of Abigail. The women's quarters were on the left side of the house. The other two servants went with Ephraim and his men to the opposite side of the house.

Sheerah was startled to round a corner and see a lovely room with flowers and burning candles. The air was redolent with wonderful scents. Sheerah couldn't get over the beauty before her. Female servants were pouring hot water into large, round tubs. The travelers gratefully stripped off their traveling garments and stepped into the soothing, warm water. Their skin responded to the warmth by getting pink in the bathing vessels, which came up to their knees. The women slipped in, with enough room to sit on the bottom. Also, as soon as they sat down, the water was dirty and needed to be replaced with clean water. Servants did this by overflowing the water so it flowed into a trough. Such extravagance she had never experienced. Sheerah didn't want the bathing to end at first, but when her mother stood up, she knew she had to leave as well.

There were satin garments for each to put on, even Naamah. Sheerah would be sorry to return to her own clothing after wearing such soft fabric. Shuai looked into all of the small earthenware jars, opening one at a time. The most delightful fragrances emanated from each jar as she opened them. Shuai showed Sheerah how to put the perfume on her arms and neck. When she anointed her wrists and neck, the smells intoxicated her, making Sheerah feel like a princess.

The servants returned and led them out of that chamber to a small, cool room at the center of the house. There were several sleeping cots, and they fell into them gratefully. Sheerah wondered if she should seek out Abigail to thank her, but sleep overtook her.

Exhausted, the women rested the day away. Sheerah came awake at dusk, concerned about her surroundings. She could not quite remember where she was. Naamah and Shuai soon woke up as well.

"I can't remember when I last slept so well," Shuai exclaimed.

Naamah nodded vigorously.

What happens next? Sheerah wondered. *I am ferociously hungry; I hope a meal is coming soon.*

Abigail soon arrived, trailed by two servants carrying large bronze trays covered with bread, cheese, and fruits.

"Please join me in a small snack, ladies," Abigail said brightly. "It is still a while until dinner is ready but I thought you all might be hungry. The men are being served in their quarters as well."

CHAPTER TWENTY-TWO

THE FIRST NIGHT of feasting was hosted by Abigail, to allow the visitors time to get situated. She spread a lavish table with meats, cheeses, fruit, and sweets. There was also plenty of wine to be shared. Midway through the festivities, Abigail rose in her place and held out her drinking vessel. She toasted Ephraim and Shuai and welcomed their entire family.

"Friends, soon-to-be neighbors, and family: Thank you for joining me and the household of Abigail for our feast tonight. I bless all present, and I confirm the covenant between our two territories. I welcome Sheerah to my family."

Abigail presented Sheerah with two new tunics of silk. One was brightly colored in a patchwork of lovely jewel tones. The other was similar, but in pastel shades.

I never dreamed I would have such beautiful clothing, she thought. *I must say something gracious, but I can not think of anything to say for such gifts.*

"I am so grateful for these wonderful gifts," she managed to stammer. Abigail smiled warmly and seemed pleased by her response. "It is my pleasure."

Sheerah and Zeruiah each sat with their own family groups, as was the custom. But Zeruiah wished they could talk. Sheerah seemed to like the tunics his mother had made for her. *Just wait. This is only the beginning of the gifts I want to shower on her,* Zeruiah thought with a smile.

The torches burned low by the time everyone finished eating and drinking, some to excess. After a glorious night of conversation and delight, Ephraim and Shuai went to their room in Abigail's spacious home, followed by Sheerah and Naamah. But they went to a different set of rooms. The servants and other members of the family eventually wandered back to their tents to sleep off the good food and drink.

The next morning dawned beautiful and hot. Shuai was muttering, fretting about the banquet she and Ephraim would host in the evening. Her main concern appeared to be that she didn't have all the bronze serving trays and utensils that Abigail had for last night's party. Ephraim reassured her that the quality of and the number of dishes she had planned would far outshine the vessels used to serve them.

Shuai was surprised by his tender words. *He must still be feeling good from last night's festivities,* she thought. Shuai decided to relax as she made preparations.

This evening's banquet lived up to Ephraim's prediction.

Everyone had a wonderful time. Zeruiah and Sheerah managed to sneak away to one side of the banquet hall for a few moments to talk. They were careful not to touch each other, but the intensity of their affection shone in their eyes. But it wasn't long until Naamah came looking for Sheerah.

Naamah came over to the couple.

"I know you will be married tomorrow night," Naamah said with some petulance, "but tonight you are still my responsibility." Sheerah and Zeruiah's actions caused Naamah to leave her seat at the celebration. She made a new friend before the banquet was finished, but Sheerah came first. Naamah steered Sheerah back to her family.

Much to Naamah's surprise, Sheerah said demurely, "I

am sorry if I spoiled your time at the banquet. Zeruiah and I haven't had time to even say 'hello' since we arrived."

Naamah's countenance softened a bit. "You'll have the rest of your lives to talk, starting tomorrow night."

Sheerah just smiled.

CHAPTER TWENTY-THREE

NAAMAH GRABBED SHEERAH's foot and shook it. From under the covers, Sheerah said, "Marumph! Let go of my foot."

Naamah replied," Get up. Your wedding is tonight!"

Sheerah said irritably, "That is tonight. Not now." She rolled in her covers and tried to go back to sleep.

Naamah grabbed her foot again, this time tickling the bottom of it.

"Okay, okay," Sheerah said, giggling, then she sat up. This time, of her own accord. "What do we need to do right now?"

Naamah thought a moment and slowly shrugged her shoulders. Sheerah scowled and acted angry, but she was teasing. She came over to give Naamah a hug and a kiss.

"You need to do your chores," Naamah said, "and leave enough time to get ready for tonight, especially for a bath."

Sheerah jumped up and started dressing, putting on a work tunic and boots. When Naamah looked quizzically at her. Sheerah said, "I need to take care of Butter. She needs good exercise this morning so she is not fractious tonight. Then she needs her feet washed and her coat groomed. I want to braid her mane and tail for the ceremony."

"All that for a horse?" Naamah teased Sheerah.

"She will be carrying the bride, you know."

"Well, you had better get started. But not until after you have some breakfast," Naamah told her. "No excuses."

Sheerah ate her morning meal very quickly and headed outside to see to Butter, who whinnied with glee when she saw Sheerah. Butter was tied to a line with some of the other horses. Sheerah grabbed the special comb and brush and worked on Butter until she shone like gold in the sunlight. When Butter objected to having her mane braided by tossing her head back and forth, Sheerah said, "Okay, but I am going to braid your tail."

Sheerah lost track of time and suddenly Naamah was calling her to lunch. *I almost forgot, Abigail will be joining us for lunch and I am a mess.* Sheerah hurried to their quarters, washed her face and hands, then put on a clean tunic. No time to redo her hair.

She raced through the halls in Abigail's house to the banquet area. She was right on time, but a knowing look from her mother made her worry that her hair wasn't right.

Lunch was wonderful with many varieties of cheeses and bread. Abigail gave Sheerah a special gift of two ornate hair combs of bronze for her hair.

"These are so beautiful," Sheerah said. "I will wear them often when I put my hair up. Thank you so much!"

Shuai and Naamah could not take their eyes off the combs. "Sheerah," Shuai said with pleasure, "you are so blessed to be joining this family!"

"Time to be getting ready," Naamah said a little tearfully. Her relationship with Sheerah would always be close, but now Sheerah needed to focus on her soon to be husband and his mother.

When they returned to their quarters, a large tub had been brought in and filled with steaming, hot water. Sheerah could hardly believe her eyes. This was much bigger than the ones she used before. *It's big enough for me to stretch my legs in. How amazing!* She wasted no time getting her clothes off and climbing into the luxurious water. This much water just for her in the desert made her feel wonderful! Female servants kept bringing in big pitchers of hot water, so she was able to soak and scrub well. She was going to be really clean. *I wonder if I can ever do this again? The perfumed soap was exquisite.* After a nice time of cleansing her body with the scents in the water, Naamah washed her hair. She rinsed it with clean water that the servants brought in.

"Okay," Naamah told Sheerah, much to her sadness, "it is time to get out. I need to do your hair."

Sheerah was wrapped in a thin blanket that covered her from head to toe. She peeked out through an opening and grinned at Naamah while the servants worked. Naamah grinned back and then proceeded to rub her hair partially dry. Once she brought Sheerah to the bed, Naamah had her sit. With great care and gentle hands, Naamah put Sheerah's curly locks into fanciful loops, curves, and braids on her head. The final touch was the addition of the hair jewelry Abigail had just given her. The combs helped to anchor the complicated style in place.

Finally, Naamah placed the frontlet Shuai had made on her head. Sheerah had decided on the pastel silk tunic and also put on a long skirt. Naamah insisted on that item for modesty. *She just has to ride that horse into the ceremony,* Naamah thought ruefully.

It will soon be time, just before sunset, when I can ride Butter into the ceremony and surprise Zeruiah, Sheerah thought. *I am so excited to see the look on his face!*

CHAPTER TWENTY-FOUR

I N A COUPLE of hours, her wedding would begin. But first, Sheerah attended a farewell tea with Shuai, Ephraim, and Naamah. Although Naamah would be staying with Sheerah, she would be only one of several ladies' maids going forward. The farewell tea was lovely with honeyed cakes, biscuits, and fresh bread that smelled incredible. The scents evoked strong memories of her younger years and Naamah's kind teaching.

"We love you so much, Sheerah," Shuai said with a tear in her eye. "You are a wonderful daughter."

"I am proud of the woman you have become, and your marriage will be of benefit to everyone," Ephraim said with a gruffness that belied the emotion in his eyes.

Naamah did not speak but cried quietly.

Eventually, Ephraim poked his head out of the tent they were using. "It's time to go to the ceremony – all the torches are lit," he reported.

"Let me see," Sheerah said. When she looked out of the tent, she was overcome. *I have never seen anything so beautiful. I am truly blessed.* "Blessed," she said aloud. *Now, where did that word come from?* she thought.

Friends, relatives, and servants stood in a huge circle, making space so everyone could see. At the center of the circle stood Zeruiah, the groom, and Abigail, his mother. Traditionally, Zeruiah's father would have had the honor of standing there, but Abigail stood in her husband's place, as she had since his death. She glowed with pride, as if her husband were standing with her, making her glow. Ephraim would soon join them, and a covenant would be solemnized this night— the two families joined, and parts of two territories exchanged.

Instead of going directly to her place in the ceremony, Sheerah headed for the horse's building, much to the embarrassment of her mother. Shuai knew that Sheerah thought about riding her horse to the ceremony. But she didn't know her daughter would go through with it. Instead of getting upset, Shuai simply shrugged her shoulders.

Inside the stable area, two strong male servants waited for Sheerah. One was holding Butter's reins. *She looks so beautiful,* Sheerah thought as she walked toward the horse. *I cannot believe she is mine. I see the servants have adjusted the pad with the straps for my feet just the way I asked. I've never seen anyone ride sideways on a horse. I will be the first!*

"My lady," said one of the servants, "are you ready?"

His statement startled her out of her thoughts. "Yes, I am," she replied happily.

Once she was hoisted onto Butter's wide back, the servants helped her get her foot into the fabric loop. She was now sitting on the padded saddle with her hidden foot loop tucked underneath. *Going to the most important night of my life with only one foot anchored to Butter. It is more modest after all. My skirt covers me down to my feet. But I can still see the sparkling anklets.*

The thoughts danced in her mind while one servant handed her Butter's reins. After receiving a glowing smile from Sheerah, both servants bowed.

"Much happiness and many blessings on this night, my lady," said the horse master.

She smiled even more broadly. *"Blessings,"* she thought,

there is that word again. I must remember to ask Zeruiah about it. I need to focus now lest I end up in the circle on my rump.

Sheerah urged Butter forward, pleased at how secure she felt in her seat. There would be a short walk before she would be with Zeruiah, this time permanently. She turned her horse, heading for the large ring of people. They were shocked. Some of them had never seen a horse, much less one carrying the bride. Sheerah and Butter rode up to the ring of guests and stopped. People swiftly moved away from the gleaming, large horse. But Zeruiah was speaking to Ephraim and did not look up right away.

When he did, and saw Sheerah and Butter, his face broke into the biggest grin Sheerah had ever seen.

She walked Butter to the center of the circle, where Ephraim waited with Zeruiah and Abigail. When she arrived there, she paused and gave her groom a proud look. Zeruiah figured out that he needed to help Sheerah get down. He went to her, took her foot out of the foot loop, and kissed her toes. Thankfully, she had made a point to keep her feet exceptionally clean. As he lowered her to the ground, he held her in his arms. She was so thankful. *That was even better than I had hoped,* she thought. *I'm so glad I did not have to be one of multiple wives of some old man.*

Zeruiah led Sheerah to a position right in front of Abigail and Ephraim. There, they performed the ceremony of joining hands. First, Zeruiah reached for her hand. Once they were joined, they each took the hand of the elder near them.

"Having joined hands and covenanted our two families together, I declare them married!" Ephraim said with enthusiasm. "It is time for the exchange of gifts. Sheerah, you may go first."

"My lord and husband, I have made you a bracelet." Sheerah handed him the gift, unwrapping it before putting it in his hand. Zeruiah stared at the gleaming bronze. *It is a precious gift to be sure,* he thought. He looked warmly into her eyes. After a touching moment between them, Zeruiah turned and clapped twice.

Into the circle came three servants, heavily laden with gifts.

The beauty and lavishness of all the gifts flabbergasted Sheerah. She did not expect this much, and the crowd roared its approval.

I need to say something! her mind seemed to scream. Finally, she found her voice. The first thing out of her mouth came out in a squeak: "All this for me?" The next thing she said was less squeaky, as she bowed to her husband and then turned to Abigail, saying, "Your acceptance of me was gift enough, and now all this? Thank you so, so much."

Zeruiah waited patiently and then urged Sheerah to come over and look more closely. She saw bronze serving vessels, and several sets of clothing, jewelry. Most lovely of all was a painting of Sheerah that Zeruiah had done from memory. She decided to forget modesty and threw her arms around Zeruiah's neck. She kissed him on the mouth in front of everyone there, to the shock of her parents and some attendees.

"Thank you," she breathed.

The crowd cheered its approval at her outward show of affection!

Shouts of "Long live Zeruiah and Sheerah," and "Many sons to be born to you," rang out as they began the celebration.

CHAPTER TWENTY-FIVE

S HEERAH AND ZERUIAH, now man and wife, walked away from the wedding circle hand in hand. He led her a short distance away to a tent decorated with colorful strips of fabric. The tent was another wonderful surprise for Sheerah. She was fascinated by the decorations since she now knew what was involved in making fabric.

Whoa! What? Sheerah thought as Zeruiah swept her off her feet and into his arms. *He is so strong!* He carried her into the tent, which was filled with beautiful pillows everywhere. He knelt and gently laid her on one of the larger ones. *Zeruiah.* gazed into her eyes, making heat rise to her cheeks. Suddenly, a raucous group outside the tent began making music and noise with some of the bronze kitchen implements.

Zeruiah stood up, smiled at Sheerah, and went to the door of the tent. A great cheer went up and then Zeruiah sent them all away. He closed the tent flap, tying it with the attached strips of cloth, and secured it with a scarlet rope. Sheerah could hear the revelers still making happy sounds as they headed back to the main group of wedding guests. She welcomed him back into her arms for their first night of married life.

    ***

At daybreak, the noisy group returned (minus a few revelers who had already passed out from drinking too much of Abigail's exceptional wine).

In the tent, the new couple were rising, full of marital joy. Zeruiah looked at Sheerah, who was about to call out. He put his finger to his lips for Sheerah to be silent. Pretty soon, the revelers gave up and went away when they got no response from inside the decorated tent.

"I am hungry, my husband," she finally said.

"Wait just a minute."

He rose and went to the corner of the tent. Carefully hidden was a wooden chest with lots of food and sweets inside. Zeruiah brought the chest over to where she was sitting, and Sheerah ravenously grabbed some dates. Zeruiah watched her eat, then just laughed at the formidable appetite his bride seemed to have developed from last night.

The rest of their wedding week, they stayed in their special tent, locked away from the rest of the world. "Thank You, God for answering my prayer to make Sheerah my bride," Zeruiah prayed delightedly while Sheerah got dressed.

All too soon, their bliss in the tent was over, and it was time to return to Abigail's home.

CHAPTER TWENTY-SIX

S HEERAH ADAPTED WELL to Abigail's household. *I am so thankful for Naamah's patient teaching,* Sheerah mused as she got accustomed to her new situation. *Naamah's insistence that I do things correctly is making it easier for me to contribute to the household now.* Abagail had many servants to do the daily chores of the household, including baking bread, which had become Sheerah's specialty. Sheerah was able to correct the household servants when they weren't doing things properly. Having had the experience of actually doing the tasks, Sheerah was an understanding leader.

She and Zeruiah had an enjoyable time with Abigail while they waited for their own home to be built. Sheerah was at their home's building site as often as she could be, learning a lot more than stacking bricks. She saw how the workers responded to the foremen, and she also saw when they were not attending to their jobs. Sometimes the foremen were cruel, beating the workers and yelling at them. Sheerah saw no reason for that. She saw that the men worked much harder on days when they received pay.

Is there a connection, she wondered?

In the meantime, the newlyweds enjoyed many sumptuous meals with Abigail. *I am so glad I will have Naamah and the other servants to help me with cooking when I get into my own home. I could never make the quality of food Zeruiah is accustomed to,* she thought.

Sheerah sat in the rooftop garden musing about her life thus far. She wondered, *why haven't I bled this moon?* Sheerah decided to wait until the next moon, and if nothing happened, she would seek out Naamah and ask her. *I miss Naamah. Even though she is around, I do not see her very much and never even just to talk. I am upset that the resentment of the household servants keeps Naamah from all but the most menial tasks. It will be different when I have my own household. My dear Naamah…* she mused as she stared off toward the horizon.

Time went by, and another moon passed without the expected bleeding. Sheerah called for Naamah, which made the other servants even more jealous and spiteful. Sheerah didn't want Naamah to suffer, but she certainly could not discuss her current dilemma with them. Sheerah decided not to mention it to her new family. For Abigail to know that her servants were not behaving well would only cause her distress.

When Naamah arrived, she was heartbreakingly glad to see Sheerah. Sheerah's trusted friend had aged in the relatively short sojourn at Abigail's home. She hugged Naamah fiercely after they were in her room, feeling her frail bones and sallow skin, and wishing there was more she could do.

"How are you?" Sheerah asked her with concern.

"I am well, my lady," Naamah said with her eyes cast down.

Sheerah took her nurse's chin in her hand, lifting her face until they were eye to eye. And then she gently asked, "Really?"

"Really," Naamah tried to reply. But as she said it, a tear betrayed her words and slid down her now wrinkled cheek.

Now I must discuss this with Zeruiah, Sheerah thought with dismay.

"How can I serve you, my lady?" Naamah said, ignoring her own tears.

"You can stop," she commanded with a kind tone in her voice. "Unless others are present, please call me Sheerah." She wiped Naamah's tears and changed the subject. "Here is what I need to know: I have not bled in two moons. Is something wrong with me?"

Naamah's shocked face scared Sheerah for a moment, but Naamah could not stop the delighted giggle that escaped from her lips. "How did we miss telling you about this?" Naamah said.

"What?" Sheerah asked, her confusion really starting to worry her.

"Sheerah!" Naamah exclaimed. "You are with child!"

CHAPTER TWENTY-SEVEN

"ZERUIAH, I HAVE something to tell you," Sheerah began when she saw him later that day. "Please come with me to the rooftop garden." When they were seated, Zeruiah turned toward her. "What is wrong, my love?" he asked, worry blooming on his face.

"Nothing is wrong," Sheerah replied. "I have very good news. I am with child!"

"Will you be alright?"

"Yes," Sheerah said, understanding Naamah's giggle from earlier. "I will be fine, and I hope to present you with a son."

Zeruiah's face still bore some anxiety, but he slowly began to smile. *I know of too many women who die in childbirth,* he thought. *I'm concerned about Sheerah's life and health. But she seems so excited and pleased.*

"I will have Naamah and my mother to help me," Sheerah said, not noticing his quiet.

I must pay attention to what Sheerah is saying, he thought. *I will speak with Ephraim, he has many children and experience in such matters.*

"Zeruiah, are you happy about the baby?" Sheerah asked, interrupting his thoughts.

"Yes, my love," he replied. "I'm just concerned for you."

Sheerah kissed him and said," I can ride a horse; I'm not like other women."

And she was right.

Sheerah's pregnancy proceeded well and peacefully. Being in her own house made her happy. She glowed with that special look that mothers-to-be often have. As the months passed, her belly grew larger and larger. Eventually, she wondered when the baby would come. Naamah told her not to rush things. She knew delivery could be difficult, especially the first time. After another few weeks, Sheerah looked like she couldn't possibly get any bigger.

One night, Sheerah felt wetness flowing from her lady parts. *Oh no,* she thought, *have I wet my bed?*

Sitting up, she called out, "Naamah, come quickly, I need you!"

Naamah had been expecting this call for some time now. In her quarters near Sheerah's room, she was ready and hurried to her charge's side.

"Naamah," Sheerah said, confused, "I have wet my bed. I am so embarrassed." Sheerah was almost in tears.

"Let me look," Naamah started to say, but when she started to speak, Sheerah clutched her belly as the first of the labor pains became evident. Naamah waited for the pain to subside. Then she lifted the covers, noting that the liquid was colorless. Confirming it wasn't urine, Naamah spoke. "There, there, love. It was your birth water breaking. You didn't wet the bed."

A while later, another birth pang came on. Naamah wet the cloth she was using on Sheerah's brow again. As dawn came, Sheerah's pains were coming very close together. Naamah didn't want to admit it, but she was becoming worried. Shuai was traveling over from Ephraim's main territory to assist her daughter, but it would be several days before she arrived. *I wonder if there is another midwife to consult with,* Naamah thought. *I attended Sheerah's birth, but I don't remember this much trouble.*

Sheerah had begun screaming with the pain of each contraction. She was on her hands and knees, in pain and out of breath. Naamah got behind her, pulling her back into a sitting position, which seemed to ease the pain somewhat. After a moment of adjustment, Sheerah was no longer screaming when the labor pains came.

The still, small voice Naamah had heard in Sheerah's childhood, spoke to Naamah's mind again. "*Pray,*" it said. Just the one word.

Pray.

So, Naamah did just that.

"O God of my master," she said, "please hear me once again. Please bring Sheerah and the baby safely through this difficult labor. I offer my life for hers. Thank you for hearing me, God of my master, Ephraim."

Suddenly, Sheerah yelped and pulled herself into a squatting position. Naamah could see the head crowning, and she swiftly got in front of Sheerah, reaching to receive the newborn. The child came soon after her hands were out.

"It's a boy!' she crowed loudly.

Zeruiah poked his head into the room from right outside the doorway. He had been there since Sheerah began screaming.

"Is Sheerah all right?" he asked with great concern.

"Yes, and your son is healthy too," Naamah said with aggravation. She had been rubbing his little chest, but the child made no sound. Just then, the newborn let out a healthy, lusty cry. Zeruiah seemed shocked by the power in his son's lungs.

Weakly, Sheerah said, "My husband, come and meet your son."

Chapter Twenty-Eight

A son? *Some men wait many years for a son. Leave it to my wonderful wife to bless me with a son so quickly.* Zeruiah was overwhelmed with joy. When Naamah handed him the child to hold, she stood close in case he dropped him. Zeruiah didn't even notice as he stared into his baby son's eyes.

"His name will be Pennah, after my father!" Zeruiah nearly shouted with confidence. Pennah let out another yell as if in response. The cry ended up shocking Zeruiah, and he quickly handed his son back to his mother.

"It is all right, my husband," said Sheerah. "He is just hungry all the time, like his father," Sheerah laughed.

The next few days were busy with the arrival of visiting relatives and well-wishers. Shuai and Abigail were delighted with their elevation to grandmother status. Ephraim visited briefly, his eyes shining with love for his favorite daughter and new grandson.

Time passed quickly and, before very long, Pennah was toddling about. It seemed he was the delight of the household. Sheerah played with Pennah often, using blocks and telling him all her dreams for building a town. She also shared her dreams of building with Zeruiah. Little Pennah either did not understand at his tiny age, or he didn't consider it a possibility. Either way, he didn't take her seriously.

All too soon, it was time to wean Pennah. Sheerah knew it was wise, but approached the rite of passage with a little sadness. Her baby was really growing up. Still, she hadn't bled this moon, and she wondered if maybe she was with child again. That was a hopeful thought.

"What is wrong this evening, Sheerah?" Zeruiah asked.

"Nothing, I..." She started hesitantly, "I have something to tell you." She lowered her eyes and said, "I am with child again, my husband."

"That's wonderful!" Zeruiah said and embraced her.

"But you said you didn't want any more children," Sheerah said, her voice full of shock and wonder at her husband's happiness.

"I only said that because of the difficulty for you, my love." He kissed her forehead. "I love Pennah," he said, "and I will love the new baby."

Sheerah's second pregnancy went very smoothly, and once again, it was time to labor and deliver her baby. This labor was nothing like the first. It was very fast, and the delivery was much easier. After what seemed like no time at all, another baby boy was born to Sheerah and Zeruiah!

"His name will be *Sheriah!*" Zeruiah announced with gusto.

CHAPTER TWENTY-NINE

O NLY A YEAR later, their world changed.
Sheerah had to turn from the window opening.
The sights and sounds of Zeruiah teaching his male servants to fight in a war made her feel anxious.

"But why do you have to go?" Sheerah had asked him the previous evening.

"The war is getting closer and closer to our territory," he replied. "We must defend our lands and especially you, my mother, and the babies as well," Zeruiah explained with a weak smile instead of his usual jovial manner. "We can't move, and they won't stop."

The fateful day arrived for Zeruiah and the servants to leave. They would need all of their training to fight the war. Sheerah shamelessly put her arms around her husband's neck in front of Abigail and the servants. She would not let go. Zeruiah finally had to peel her arms from him. He kissed her once, deeply, and then he and the servants left. Sheerah watched with tears streaming down her face until they disappeared over the horizon. Abigail was crying also, and hugged her daughter-in-law fiercely. After her embrace, Abigail started coughing again.

It sounded to Sheerah like the cough was getting worse.

"Are you all right?" Sheerah asked, concerned.

"Yes, my dear, I will be fine."

Sheerah had her doubts. She resolved to speak with Naamah about Abigail's condition immediately. She sent for her, and soon, there was a knock on her door.

"Milady, you sent for me?" Naamah said quietly.

"Oh yes, Naamah, come right in. I've made tea." Sheerah's voice sounded shaky. "I am worried about Abigail," she said as she sipped. "Her coughing is getting worse and more and more frequent. What can we do for her?"

"I heard that she was ill," said Naamah. "I do not know of any remedy. We could give her honey to ease her throat, but beyond that, I don't know."

"Abigail insists that she will be fine. I doubt she would want us to call a doctor, but I'll ask her."

"We must pray to the God of Ephraim and ask for help, just like I did when you were bitten by the snake and when we were lost in the sandstorm. He helped us both times.

"How do I address Him, what do I call Him?" Sheerah said, curious.

"I just called to Him as the 'God of my master, Ephraim,'" Naamah explained.

"Okay, let's pray together." Sheerah said, and then began, "God of my father Ephraim, please heal Abigail's cough. It wracks her body and keeps her from sleeping. Please make her better." She looked at Naamah. "Now what do we do?"

"Now we wait," Naamah said simply.

Chapter Thirty

"A BIGAIL, PLEASE LET me call the doctor to come see you," Sheerah requested.

"No," Abigail said, breathing hard from a coughing spell. "I will be fine. Don't worry about me. Just look after those two beautiful boys." She looked at her grandsons. "Pennah is beginning to look just like Zeruiah, don't you think?"

Just like Abigail, trying to distract me from my concern by talking about one of my favorite subjects.

"The boys are doing well," Sheerah said, "though sometimes Pennah takes advantage of younger Sheriah when they wrestle. I wish their father were here to help with the discipline, but they are good boys."

One day, a messenger arrived at Ephraim's home. "I have news from the war," he said breathlessly.

Ephraim motioned to a servant to bring water to the thirsty messenger. After drinking deeply, the messenger was able to speak. "Your servants acquit themselves well, milord. And none have been lost."

"And my son-in-law?"

"Doing very well, milord. He has proven to be an excellent commander."

"That is particularly good news. Please have a meal and then take this news to my daughter."

"Yes, milord, and thank you."

Meanwhile, Sheerah's household was in an uproar. One of Sheerah's maids was delighted to hear of the messenger's arrival at Ephraim's home. The messenger was her betrothed. But for Sheerah, it was not joyful. She fretted at the delay. *Surely*, she thought, *Zeruiah must be all right*. She reasoned that all must be well, or her father would have sent the messenger to her right away.

Eventually, the messenger arrived at Sheerah's house.

"Come in, come in," Sheerah said impatiently. "Do you have news of my husband?"

"Yes, lady, I do. He is an able commander, and the men greatly respect him. You should be very proud of him. He is well."

Sheerah's knees became so weak with relief that she almost fell down right where she stood.

"Thank you so, so much," she said. "If you see him, tell him his wife loves him and misses him terribly." She turned to her sons. "You boys behave, I must go see your grandmother."

When she arrived, Sheerah could hear Abigail's painful cough before she came through the door. She was shocked at how gaunt Abigail had become since the last time she saw her two months ago.. Sheerah spoke to the servants, "Get some broth for milady, right now."

The servants hurried away to do Sheerah's bidding. They, too, were concerned for their mistress. Abigail was a shadow of the vibrant woman she had been only months ago.

"I'm sending for the doctor," Sheerah said firmly. This time, there was no objection from Abigail. That in itself worried Sheerah. Sheerah sent a servant to fetch the doctor.

CHAPTER THIRTY-ONE

T HE DOCTOR ARRIVED within the hour. He seemed shocked by Abigail's appearance but went right to work, first listening to her breathing by placing his ear to Abigail's chest. As he listened, the doctor's eyes grew sad. Abigail's breathing was ragged, and her cough nearly constant while the doctor performed his examination. Once done, the doctor started rummaging through his dirty sack. He found what he was looking for and held it up. It looked to Sheerah like a vial of leaves and dirt. Receiving a bowl from a servant, the doctor poured some of the leaf-dirt mixture into it. He went to the fireplace and grabbed a small stick, then set the leaves on fire. They burned, but the smell was not unpleasant.

"This will ease her breathing and her cough," he said. "Do it every day."

"Will this cure the sickness?" Sheerah inquired.

The doctor shook his head sadly and said quietly, "There is no cure. I am sorry."

Sheerah was devastated. *I was so sure the doctor would help Abigail, I thought. Now what will I do? I must continue to run both my household and hers and visit with Abigail more often.*

The leaves seemed to be doing some good, and Abigail was

able to rest and breathe with less effort. Sheerah was sad as she left to check on her sons. *I need a hug.*

When she reached her home and saw her sons, her mood lifted. She asked for and received a hug from each of them.

"How is Grandmother Abigail?" Pennah asked.

Tears slipped down Sheerah's cheek as she answered, "She is very sick and may be dying." She thought, *This feels like I am losing my own mother.* Abigail had always been so kind to her, helping her set up her household and raise her sons. *I can't imagine life without her.*

Sheerah visited Abigail often, sometimes bringing Pennah and Sheriah with her. Sheriah remained very sad and had a tough time with the visits. One day, Abigail insisted on having a scribe come to the house. She spent a lot of time with the scribe, since her coughing fits often greatly interfered with conversation. Finally, she was done, and the scribe left. She called Sheerah in and handed her the clay tablet.

"What is this?"

"This is a document giving you and Zeruiah, my house and worldly goods. If Zeruiah doesn't return, it all goes to you. The scribe was confused because he had never executed an agreement giving a woman an inheritance."

Sheerah didn't know what to say. She had heard of widowed daughters-in-law being thrown out of the family home and left destitute. *I have tried not to think about it much, or I would be crazy with pain and fear,* Sheerah pondered. But, to not only keep her in the main family home *and* give it to her and Zeruiah was unheard of. Sheerah was flabbergasted.

A month later, she visited Abigail. Reaching her quarters, Sheerah was lighthearted but solemn. She was slightly alarmed by the absence of coughing noise, and she ran to Abigail, dropping to her side.

Abigail's body was lifeless, but a peaceful smile rested upon her lips.

Abigail gone? Sheerah's mind screamed at her. *How can this be?*

She began to sob as reality set in. *I have no idea what to do for her funeral. We never discussed it. I didn't want to believe it would happen. I'll send an urgent message to my mother and ask her to come help.*

But for just a moment, Sheerah let her tears flow freely over her beloved Abigail.

CHAPTER THIRTY-TWO

S HUAI ARRIVED A week later. She knew how special Abigail
was to her daughter.

*The excarnation period, leaving the body protected but open
to the air, should be nearly finished,* Shuai thought. *I wonder
where her husband's burial mound is located. Despite the sad
reason for my visit, I'm so excited to see Sheerah.*

Shuai went to the main part of the house. Just as she
entered, Sheerah saw her and squealed with delight at the sight
of her mother.

"Eema, I am so glad to see you!" she exclaimed.

The women hugged long and hard.

"I am sorry for the reason," Shuai said with happy tears,
"but I am so happy to see you."

Shuai had been correct; the excarnation period was almost
over. It was soon time to get Abigail's body ready for burial.
Over the next few days, Sheerah and Shuai planned what they
could. Sheerah showed her mother all of Abigail's favorite
clothing and jewelry, pointing out the ones Abigail wore a lot.
They dressed her body in her favorite tunic with a special silk
scarf. Sheerah chose decadent jewelry for her neck and wrists,
with more of her favorite pieces placed in her hands. Abigail
looked beautiful in spite of the decay affecting her body. Finally,

the burial shroud was placed around her form. She would be buried in the family burial mound.

Sheerah was devastated.

Over the course of a few days, the servants excavated the burial mound of Abigail's husband. They cleared it all the way back to the chamber that held her husband's body and those of his parents. Those same servants would carry Abigail's body to the chamber and replace the soil during that part of the burial ceremony. When finished, they would replace the grassy pieces they had removed prior to the excavation.

Shuai remained with Sheerah throughout the mourning month. She was reluctant to leave her daughter, but knew Sheerah needed to find her own way of handling the responsibilities of her inheritance. Shuai certainly hoped Zeruiah would be home soon and wondered if the young man even knew of his mother's death.

In her alone time, Sheerah found herself manipulating the blocks she had asked the servants to carve for her sons. When she couldn't sleep, she would get the blocks from her sons' rooms and play with ideas. She built many different structures while she thought about what she might do to honor Abigail's memory.

How do I honor such a strong woman? she thought.

Chapter Thirty-Three

Years passed.

Sheerah's sons were thirteen years old and sixteen. They were men making their way in the world. One night in the warmer months, Sheerah invited them for a meal. They would be joined by Pennah's betrothed.

"As you know," she began at their banquet, "I have wanted to do something to memorialize the life of Abigail. You are also aware that I have a desire to build. I have decided, with your help, to build a town at Upper Beth Horon."

There was silence around the table as the young people looked from one to another. Sheriah found his voice first.

"Mother," he said, "you know only men build cities."

"That is why I need your assistance," she replied with a calm smile. "I have the finances to cover everything. I want to pay you both and hire workers, buy supplies, oh, and donkeys to carry them. I will provide all the designs and plans for an entire village."

Neither of Sheerah's sons knew what to say. It was shocking news. Pennah already had a household and a future wife to provide for. But since there was pay involved, he could potentially leave his flocks and herds with a professional shepherd. He could still be involved.

Shemiah was freer in his time due to his younger age. He eagerly assented to the plan. *Could this even be done?* he thought. *What would the people around them think and say? I do not want Mother to fail. But when has Mother ever failed?* He chided himself.

Once the food was cleared, Sheerah clapped twice and servants bearing clay tablets came into the room. They put them down on the table with a thump. Each one of them was dry and had markings on them; some on both sides. Sheerah arranged them just so for Pennah and Shemiah, who were amazed to see the map. They looked in awe at the main and smaller roads, which were marked with various buildings sketched in.

"How long have you been working on this?" Shemiah asked. Pennah nodded, adding his curiosity to his brother's question.

Sheerah smiled at her sons with a twinkle in her eye and said, "Quite some time now."

They began to pepper her with questions in tandem.

"When do you want to start?"

"Has the property been arranged for?"

"Are there any residents?"

"What shall we do about them?"

"What about building materials?"

Sheerah smiled at her sons' questions. *And I was worried about convincing them,* she thought. Most of the questions she had answers for, since she had been considering this for a long time—*since childhood,* she thought.

"I want to start as soon as possible," Sheerah explained. "I have made an agreement to purchase the land that is now a small village of a few homes. I thought we might buy them or help the owners improve the homes as they wish."

"Did Grandmother Abigail really leave us enough to do this well?" Pennah asked.

Just like her firstborn to be concerned about such things, Sheerah thought with a smile.

"Yes, she did. In fact, I am planning other villages as well."

"Maybe we should see how the first one goes," her pragmatic second-born suggested.

"If we are agreed, let's go visit the property tomorrow and finalize the sale."

CHAPTER THIRTY-FOUR

THE PROJECT MOVED forward rapidly from that point. Pennah and Shemiah hired workers, but everyone was aware they were laboring for Sheerah. Her generosity caused her name to become famous in the area.

Not everyone was happy to hear it.

Sheerah's neighbors gossiped. Their jealousy and fear of anything new led them to tell tales and falsehoods about Sheerah. Some of the men were threatened by Sheerah's success. But the people already dwelling on the property were impressed with her giving nature and her good sense of planning. Several of them chose to sell, but most of them were happy to accept her offer to help them improve their properties.

First, a wall went up to surround the entire village. This was the biggest and most expensive part of the project. Sheerah inspected the work daily on horseback. She was friendly with the workers and residents who were helping, but she did not hesitate to correct things that were not done to her exacting standards. The walls were comprised of stacked bricks with a thin layer of sand acting as a mordant. The bricks varied in length so that all the joinings would be covered with at least one stone, making the wall stronger. There was an opening flanked by large, rectangular, carved stones placed on end, which was created for entry to the town.

Inside the wall, workers built simple houses in assorted sizes. They were built after the usual pattern of the day, with a lower level for animals and storage, and an upper level for family life. But Sheerah improved on that design. The difference in the homes Sheerah built was an abundance of terraces extending from the upper stories over an extended lower story. This was a new concept for the buildings of the era. No one had thought of individual homes having the luxury of an outdoor living space for plants and sleeping in the hot months.

Sheerah was as happy as she could remember, seeing her dreams come to life. But then a shadow crossed her mind, *how I wish Zeruiah were here to share this with me.* Tears slipped from her eyes. *I must be strong like Abigail was. She lived a good portion of her life without her husband. She did very well for herself and gave to those in need. Abigail was able to give such a substantial inheritance to Sheerah, and Zeruiah never knew.* More tears fell at the thought of her beloved.

Growing up with Abigail's ideas and attitudes, Zeruiah developed a supportive way of looking at Sheerah's projects. His mother's unconventional way of doing business and managing her wealth was not lost on her son, and he always encouraged Sheerah to follow her dreams. His loss in the war was almost unbearable for Sheerah sometimes.

Sheerah decided to throw a party to celebrate the completion of the wall. There was still much to be done, but Sheerah wanted to celebrate the great progress with the workers and residents. She chose a day and had the servants help get bread, meat, honeyed dates, and other sweets ready for the party. She wanted it to be a surprise, so she waited for the day's work to be finished and met the workers as they left the site. Tables full of delectable foods and wine were quickly set up by the servants at the work site, and everyone enjoyed themselves. *I think Abigail would be pleased,* Sheerah thought. *I'm glad she taught me how much pleasure is derived from serving and entertaining others.*

The following day, all the workers went back to working on the houses, shops, and meeting places. But word spread about the celebration and the great treatment. Very soon after the party for the wall, people from the surrounding areas were clamoring to purchase homes and shops.

Sheerah consulted her sons about the sales once she heard about the increased interest.

"The income that comes in, including the herds and flocks, will be used for the next village. But before we start accepting payments, I want each of you to choose a home for yourselves," Sheerah said with a smile.

They had all learned a great deal about village building from the process of building Upper Beth Horon. The next village, Lower Beth Horon, was built much more quickly, since there was no shortage of workers wanting to be employed by Sheerah. The two villages were joined by a road, and lots of commerce moved along it. Even the caravans of Sheerah's youth became regular visitors.

Over time, the shops and marketplaces became filled with brilliant-colored silks, spices, jewels, special foodstuffs, and everyday needs. Her towns were successful, and the inhabitants profited from that success.

Sheerah's fame as a builder grew.

Mouth to mouth, the workers spread stories about her generosity and valuable new designs. A woman building cities, who would have imagined such a thing? But her talent could not be denied. Even tribal leaders sought her wisdom.

CHAPTER THIRTY-FIVE

WHEN NAAMAH DIED, a year after the second town began construction, Sheerah mourned the loss acutely. Her beloved servant and friend, teacher of all Sheerah needed to know to run a household, died at a good, old age after a protracted illness. Sheerah had her dear nurse buried near the family burial mound in a place of honor and shook off her sadness with difficulty.

But she had to.

Pennah's wedding was on the horizon, and Shemiah was about to be betrothed.

I miss my husband so much, Sheerah thought. *I thought his loss would be easier as time went on, but it hasn't been. I still cannot believe that I will never see him again.* The tears flowed anew. She heard Pennah's voice on the first floor of her home and started to worry he might see her cry. *This is a happy time for him,* she thought as she quickly dried the tears from her cheeks.

As a prominent family, the wedding would be large and sumptuous. Surrounding area neighbors were anxiously awaiting the big event. *I must forgive them for their nasty gossiping about my towns so that Pennah's wedding can be a thoroughly happy occasion.*

"Eema!" Sheniah and Pennah called simultaneously.

"Up here, boys," she called back, grinning, since she knew they hated to be called "boys."

"I am blessed to see both of you," she greeted them as they entered her room.

Pennah, since he was older *and* the groom, had been doing most of the wedding planning.

"Eema, may we use one of the horses for Hadassah to ride into the ceremony as you did?" Pennah had heard tales of his parents' wedding for many years and from many people.

"Yes. You may, if you teach her to ride safely."

"Already taken care of!" Pennah smiled.

"I think a merchant caravan will be coming through during the week of the wedding. That will make the event even more festive," Pennah continued.

A thought occurred to Sheerah: *I must remember to go to the slave traders' caravan and get some more servants for the wedding before the slave traders caravan moves on. They will be doing that soon.*

"Eema, are you listening?" Sheniah said. "All this wedding talk makes me eager to be betrothed to Mirami.

"I will arrange a meeting with Mirami's parents as soon as your brother's wedding festivities are concluded."

Shemiah was exasperated. "I know, I know, I am the younger brother. I must wait."

"You are also young in age, barely a man. Your time will come, I promise," Sheerah said.. Shemiah *looks so much like his father. How I miss him, but I mustn't cry.*

Sheerah left early the next morning with her trusted servants to go to the slave traders' caravan to find some more slaves. She chose three strong-looking, burly men and two women. Prices were negotiated, and the servants would be delivered to Sheerah's home, where the traders would receive their pay.

As she turned her horse back to her property, she heard that small, quiet voice in her head saying, "Look again, look again."

Look at what? she thought. But she turned her horse back towards the caravan just in time to see one of the slaves smiling. *What does he have to smile about,* she wondered curiously. The smile quickly faded, but Sheerah had made up her mind to purchase the smiling slave. The traders were always anxious to make another sale. Out of the corner of her eye, Sheerah saw the foreman raise his lash.

"Don't you touch my servant!" Sheerah's commanding voice stopped him mid-stroke. And that slave was placed with the other servants Sheerah purchased.

"Treat them kindly or I will not pay you." She left two of her trusted servants to monitor the traders' behavior during the trip to her house. The servants were delivered without incident on the agreed-upon date. They lined up in the yard for Sheerah's inspection. She assigned each of the men to a trusted attendant to be fed, washed, and to learn their tasks.

The face of the "smiling slave" haunted Sheerah, but she did not know why. He kept his eyes appropriately downcast and did not look directly at her.

That smile, Sheerah thought. *There's something about that smile…*

CHAPTER THIRTY-SIX

T HE PREPARATIONS FOR Pennah's wedding were proceeding at a breakneck pace. The merchants' caravan arrived as expected with food, decorations, gifts, and other nice items. Wedding attire was prepared, and the ovens spread wonderful aromas through the yard and house. The bride-to-be, Hadassah, had moved into Sheerah's house to learn the ways and protocols of the household (just as Sheerah had done with Abigail).

The two women enjoyed spending time together.

On the day of the wedding, there were cloudless, blue skies. People from all around were delighted at the caravan and its wares, and the beautiful weather helped everyone's mood stay high. Hadassah came to the wedding circle on horseback, just as Sheerah had on her wedding day. And after being helped from the horse by her groom, Pennah, the wedding took place. Now it was time for the feasting and dancing, and Sheerah looked on with approval.

Suddenly, she caught a glimpse of someone who looked just like Zeruiah. She shook her head and blinked her eyes. The next second, she did not see him. *My mind is imagining things because I would so love for my husband to be here.*

The festivities continued into the night. At some point, a

servant was at her elbow to pour her more wine. She looked up with a smile and then screamed and fainted into the arms of Zeruiah, the "smiling slave."

Sheerah's attendants rushed over to protect her, but by the time they arrived, she was smiling ear to ear. It *was* her beloved husband, whom she thought had died in the war.

He carried her to her room so they could speak privately. But before she spoke, she kissed him fiercely.

"Why didn't you speak up in the caravan when I first came to purchase more servants?" she asked when she finally released him.

"I was not sure how you would receive me," he said hesitantly, "now that I am a slave."

"I did not recognize you under all the dirt and the scars," she said, starting to weep. "But I love you! And I did not forget you, even when I thought you were dead."

Zeruiah and Sheerah were interrupted by the tent door flying open. Shemiah rushed to his mother's room, wanting to check on her after her fainting spell. He stopped short when he saw her being held by a servant.

"Shemiah," Sheerah said with a grin, "come and meet your father."

"Zeruiah?" Shemiah asked with astonishment.

"Son," Zeruiah said quietly, "I do not really expect that you would remember me. I left for the war when you were very young."

Shemiah looked dumbfounded by this admission. But then he decided his mother would know Zeruiah best. Rather than speak to him, Shemiah ran out of the tent quickly to find his brother.

Sheerah made sure that proper clothes were available for Zeruiah and the household servants were informed of the change in status of the "smiling slave."

Despite it being Pennah's wedding, it was as if Sheerah

was a new bride again. They took great joy in reconnecting as a family, and many nights of tales followed the wedding. Zeruiah told of his adventures fighting the war and how he was captured and sold as a slave.

One day, Sheerah said, "I have a surprise for you. The horses are waiting in the yard." They rode out laughing and were soon climbing the crest of a hill. A lovely valley stretched out beneath them.

"Beautiful," Zeruiah breathed. "Whose land is this?"

"It is ours, Beloved. Welcome to what will be the town of Uzzam-Sheerah."

THE END

EPILOGUE

T HE TOWNS BUILT by Sheerah are mentioned in other places in Scripture. Joshua 10:10 tells us that Joshua and the Israelites pursued the Amorites up the road to Beth Horon after defeating them at Gibeon. This is the area where the miracle of the sun not setting for an extra day occurred. Joshua 16:1-3 tells of the allotment of the promised land for Joseph and his tribe. One of the boundaries was the region of Lower Beth Horon. Ephraim and Manasseh each had their territory carved from Joseph's allotment. One of the towns given to the Kohathite clan of Levites from Ephraim's territory included Beth Horon and its surrounding areas (Joshua 21:21). I Samuel 13:18 relates that the Philistine army sent raiding parties toward Beth Horon. II Chronicles 8:5 tells us that Solomon rebuilt and fortified Upper Beth Horon and Lower Beth Horon.

Upper and Lower Beth Horon still exist today. They are identified as the Palestinian villages of Beit Ur al-Fauqa and Beit Ur al-Tahta, respectively.

This novel was enormous fun to research and write. I hope you enjoyed reading it. May God richly bless you!

CJS January 5, 2024

ABOUT THE AUTHOR

FINALLY ABLE TO indulge in a lifelong love for writing after retirement from forty years as a Clinical Laboratory Scientist, Christ follower C.J. Scott now resides in Carlsbad, California. She enjoys reading, researching, writing, and has an avocation for archaeology. Her family is a joy, and she loves spending time with her two sons, their wives, and her grandchildren, Sophia and Jordan, as well as her family of origin and Mom, who is a healthy 99-year-old. C.J. is very involved in the international Kingdom Writers Association, heading up the Oceanside, California chapter.

Contact: saundra53@gmail.com

TIARA PUBLISHING